THE

DUKE

OF D.C.

THE DUKE OF D.C.

JAMES MOSELEY

FRANKLIN GREEN
PUBLISHING
franklingreenpublishing.com

The Duke of D.C.
The American Dream
By James Allen Moseley

Franklin Green Publishing
232 South St
Concord NH 03301
franklingreenpublishing.com

International Standard Book Number: 978-1-936487-52-3

Editing: Heidi Jensen

Cover/Interior design by Kent Jensen | knail.com

Cover Ship photo: Wikimedia Commons, United States public domain

Cover Coins photo: Wikimedia Commons, Creative Commons license

Cover Washington Monument photo: Unsplash.com

CONTENTS

DEDICATION

To Madlene, who, on our wedding day,
Vowed to back my writing in every way.
In triumph or failure, hope or despair,
In tempest or calm, she was always there
To shelter and kindle my dreams, and now
She has more than fulfilled her wedding vow.

— and —

To President Donald J. Trump, a man of genius, talent,
courage, generosity, and vision, who has done more to
"Make America Great Again" than any president in our history
and even more than the American Duke.

CREDITS

Story by James Moseley.
Narration by James Moseley.
Music by James Moseley.
Lyrics by James Moseley.
Director: James Moseley.
A James Moseley Production.

HISTORICAL NOTE

This narrative contains conscious anachronisms. For example, the author is well aware that Lafayette was not yet in America by the date on which he appears in this story. However, in fiction, as Sir Arthur Conan Doyle once remarked, sometimes these things happen.

Part One

Politics is the art of looking for trouble,
finding it everywhere, diagnosing it incorrectly,
and applying the wrong remedies.

—Groucho Marx

CHAPTER 1

PUBLISH
OR PERISH

"I am attractive," said Professor Ilsa Guilford-Schlitz, preening thoughtfully in her compact mirror, "in a scholarly sort of way." She was, in fact, prettier than she gave herself credit for. She had rich, silky brown hair, a snowy complexion, shapely lips, large, hazel eyes that always seemed to reflect mild astonishment, and a trim, charmingly feminine form. Her insecurity came not from any deficiency in her appearance, but from an ever-present, subconscious undertow of anxiety. She had acquired this from all her years of study. She was always afraid of failing grades, although in fact when earning both her master's degree and her Ph.D., she had attained consistently high marks. However, her mountain of student debt loomed darkly in the back of her mind, and the discovery, upon graduation, that a doctorate in history was no guarantee of profitable employment, did nothing to inspire a feeling of bravado. She had, fortunately, landed a professorship at a leading D.C. university, and she hoped dearly to qualify for tenure. So nothing was ever really as worrisome as Ilsa tended to believe, but worry she did, and this was the reason why, from time to time, she gave herself little pep talks while gazing into her compact mirror.

"Intelligent, too," she told herself, trying to conjure up conviction. She snapped the mirror shut and glanced at her watch. Nine forty. Ah. Well, there was, perhaps, reason for a touch of concern. At ten o'clock her department head, Dean Bradford M. Bradford, had booked an official appointment with her. With Bradford, it was always official, and official meant ominous. Ilsa grabbed her purse, a yellow pad, and a pen and left her cubicle. Conscious of the seconds ticking, she sprinted to Bradford's office. A heel broke off one of her shoes. On the run, she stooped like a ball boy at Wimbledon to snatch it up. She tucked it into her purse and limped unevenly as she entered the anteroom of the dean's lair. In it was a cramped desk with a sour secretary huddled over it, rather like a malevolent sphinx at the gate of Thebes.

"You're late," said the secretary, nodding toward Bradford's door.

In his magnificent, walnut-paneled office, Bradford M. Bradford paced around his massive desk impatiently, thinking to himself, "She cometh not." But then the door swung open, and Ilsa's shoes sunk into thick, luxurious carpeting, one shoe a little more deeply than the other, and she coughed slightly, like a hesitant sheep, before speaking. "Ahem. Dr. Bradford..."

Bradford held up a skinny, admonitory hand. He was a tall, slender man with sloping shoulders, eyebrows that looked like two caterpillars on a collision course above his beaky nose, a bald dome, and a piercing gaze that could open an oyster at twenty paces.

"*Dr. Dr.* Bradford, if you please," he said, correcting Ilsa. "I earned a double Ph.D., and it does not do to hide one's lamp beneath a basket!"

"Sorry, Dr. Dr.," gulped Ilsa.

"I suppose you know why I have called you in."

"Yes, sir. My paper."

"Or, to be more precise," he said archly, "your lack of one. You know, the university requires that professors on a tenure track do more than teach. You are, supposedly, on a track to tenure, am I right?"

"That is my hope," gulped Ilsa.

"Well, to elevate your prospects above mere hope, m'girl, you must publish some innovative or ingenious theory or thesis or study in the academic press at least once per year."

"Well..."

"But you have not," he said, interrupting her, "met the publishing requirements, Dr. Guilford-Schlitz." He sighed and gazed up at the ornamental ceiling of his majestic office. "We all had such high hopes when you joined us at the university, but now..."

"My students all give me good reviews."

Bradford shot her a look that sliced like a bullet searing through butter.

"Students, Dr. Guilford-Schlitz, do not bring the university endowments or prestige. If you want to rise in academia, making the institution look good is your key concern."

Ilsa gulped. "You mean...?"

"Publish or perish, Dr. Guilford-Schlitz. It's the unwritten law of the academic jungle." And with that, to Ilsa's astonishment, Dr. Dr. Bradford M. Bradford broke into a tango melody, to which he also danced with a blend of gravitas and flair. He sang in a pleasant, light baritone.

SONG: *PUBLISH OR PERISH*

Bradford: A tenured position, you know, is forever,
A wonderful thing to possess.
You needn't work hard or be terribly clever,
And you'll never be ousted, unless...

"Unless?" asked Ilsa nervously.

Bradford: You fail to live up to just one little rule,
The guideline that all the trustees cherish,
That *sine qua non* that brings funds to school—
Professors must publish or perish!

"But what about," said Ilsa, "the study I made on the aerodynamics of Native American arrowheads?"

"I seem to remember we had to hush that up," said Bradford. "Your experiment shooting them over the football field brought down the Goodyear blimp. It cost the university a fortune in insurance premiums."

"Yes, but the arrowheads were awfully aerodynamic," said Ilsa hopefully.

"No, doctor," said Bradford, "we need something that brings money in, not blows it out." He then resumed his menacing song and dance.

Bradford: Publish or perish, it's a weary dance
That every academic has to do.
Come up with something novel; it's your only chance:
Some theory or some thesis, or you're through.

The mystifying magic of the published word
Makes the donor dollars tumble in.
Publish, and your tenure here will be assured.

Perish, and, alas, what might have been!

Swept away by the awful threats, Ilsa also responded in song, but she didn't dance, at least not yet.

> Ilsa: You know, sir, I've tried sir,
> I've searched far and wide, sir,
> For a thesis that would win a hefty grant.
> But whatever I do, sir,
> It just won't come through, sir,
> I wish that I could do it, but I can't.

"Can't?" spluttered Bradford.

> Ilsa: Please don't let me perish!
> This post that I cherish
> Is the only thing that I know how to do.
> Though my future is bearish,
> And to grovel is garish,
> Please give me another chance or two!

On his willowy legs, Bradford advanced toward Ilsa, took one of her hands in his, put his other hand on her waist, and began to lead her in a tango around the room, as both of them continued the song.

> Bradford: Publish or perish, what a price to pay!

> Ilsa: Writing isn't really what I do.
> Unlocking mystery in history is my *forte*.

> Bradford: That's a rather backward-looking point of view.
> Publish or perish; it's a rigid law.

> Ilsa: Can't you give me just a bit more time?

Bradford: I'll give you thirty days, but that's your last hurrah!
Thirty days and then the bells will chime.

Both: Publish or perish; it's an iron rule!

Ilsa: What will I come up with, I wonder?

Bradford: It's the major means of propping up the dear, old
school.

Both: It's the guillotine professors must live under!

Just as the tangoing duo spun to a tableau finish, the sour
secretary poked her head around the door. She goggled at the sight.
"*Olé,*" concluded Bradford with a flourish.

CHAPTER 2

THE CAPITOL RIOT

Ray Almaviva was a dapper, young professor of political science at another leading D.C. university. Unlike Ilsa, he had tenure, and his confident demeanor betrayed it. His Hispanic charm, dashing mustache and all, was reminiscent of the actor Don Ameche when he was young. Ray was a bon vivant, boulevardier, and raconteur, the kind of person everyone liked, especially female students. The number of female students who had majored in political science since he had become head of the department had excited considerable comment on campus. But that wasn't what was on his mind.

Today Ray was brimming with more than his usual vim because it was a momentous day. For political science, that is. It was, in point of fact, January 6, 2021, and thousands of protestors from all around the country were converging on Washington, D.C., to protest allegations of fraud in the recent presidential election. Not that Ray was an activist. Far from it. But he was an avid student of politics and polls; and he was eager to witness what would transpire when the crowds reached their stated destination, Capitol Hill.

The weather was overcast with light rain and 37 degrees Fahrenheit at high noon. Not lovely, but invigorating. Ray liked walking in D.C. It gave him a chance to treat attractive female pedestrians with a good look at him. And, of course, he was far from averse to looking at them. His path today took him past Union Station, out of which were pouring hundreds, maybe thousands, of people, attired in red baseball caps and carrying placards. Ray approached one of the protestors, a kind-looking middle-aged woman.

"What's going on?" he asked, as if he didn't know.

"We're going to the Capitol," said the woman. "To stop the steal."

"The steal?" asked Ray.

"Yeah, the fake elections," said the kind-looking woman's husband. "If we don't have election security, we don't have a country. Want to join us?"

"I'll catch you there," said Ray. He knew what it would be like if he joined the mob: chaos. Sweaty masses. Police cordons. Bull horns. Yes, it was a movement. But a mess. Something to discuss in a future lecture. But one needed to keep the impartial perspective of an academic observer.

As Ray walked along Pennsylvania Avenue, the crowds became denser and denser as they approached the Capitol, until on the Hill, he found he couldn't avoid swimming in a sea of humanity.

The protestors were carrying American flags, wearing red "Make America Great Again" caps, and brandishing signs with such slogans as "Stop the Steal," "Save America," and "Guilty of Loving My Country." The crowd had swarmed up the Capitol steps and onto the balcony, but even though passions were running high, the scene was, as a whole, civilized.

Suddenly, a brawny man with a red baseball cap in a camouflage tunic stood out from the crowd. He began yelling, with his beefy hands cupped to his mouth, "We need to go into the Capitol! Let's go!"

Many of the protesters shouted back, "No! No!"

But the brawny man shouted all the louder, "Into the Capitol! Let's go!"

Some of the protestors pointed at the brawny man and shouted, "That guy's a Fed! Fed! Fed! Fed! Fed!"

The brawny man suddenly turned to Ray. "You need to go in," he said.

"Why?" asked Ray.

The brawny man put his face, twisted with passion, close to Ray's nose. "Do you love your country?" he snarled.

"What's that got to do with it?" asked Ray.

"Go in!" shouted the brawny man.

"*I'm* not *going into the Capitol,*" said Ray. "Are you nuts?"

The brawny man snarled and turned away. Just then, Ray noticed that a television reporter from WONK-TV, Monica Bingley, had captured his brief conversation with the brawny man on camera. Ray smiled and waved at her and her cameraman and moved along. The brawny man, however, who seemed to be everywhere at once, began to shout again and again, "Into the Capitol! Into the Capitol! All of you! In!" And, shoving several protestors from behind, he began to move them along like cattle being prodded into a stampede. A knot of people holding placards and American flags closed in on Ray and jostled him forward.

"Excuse me," said Ray, trying to extricate himself.

But the brawny man kept shouting, "Into the Capitol!" and continued to push. Ray was swept up the Capitol steps in a human tsunami. When he reached the doors, the Capitol police stood placidly to one side while the brawny man, who had somehow slipped to the front of the crowd, opened the doors and again shouted, "Into the Capitol!" Ray was the first to get shoved inside.

"All right, I'm going in. Satisfied?" Ray said in exasperation. For a suffocating few seconds, he was sandwiched between a gaggle of protesters. Then, once indoors, the protesters spread out and began milling around placidly. They strolled about the Capitol like tourists, respectfully picking up brochures and taking photos of the statues and architecture. "This is sort of fascinating, from a poly sci point of view," thought Ray.

Then a man burst upon the scene wearing body paint, no shirt, a Viking helmet with horns, and brandishing an American flag. Ray laughed, and the good-natured, would-be shaman ambled over to him.

"What are you supposed to be?" asked Ray. "A Q-Anon Shaman?"

"Could be," said the man with the Viking helmet. He affably shook Ray's hand. Then he sauntered casually through the Capitol, flanked by genial Capitol police, who opened a door for him. He bowed at their gracious gesture and disappeared through the door.

Ray had seen enough. It was time to get back outside. As he wandered toward the exit, the crowds began rooting in enthusiastic unison, "USA! USA! USA!" Their chanting echoed in the rotunda.

Ray made his way back down the Capitol steps and plunged through the crowd outside, which was much larger and more boisterous than the curious tourists inside the building. Just then, WONK-TV reporter Monica Bingley and her cameraman zoomed in on Ray.

"May we have a word?" she asked.

"Sure," said Ray.

"You were inside?" she asked.

"Yep," said Ray. "Nothing much to see."

"Hundreds of protestors and nothing to see? Isn't this an assault on our democracy? A threat to our Constitution?"

"Oh, I wouldn't say *it's an assault on our democracy*. I also wouldn't say *it's a threat to our Constitution*. It's just protesters. We have them in D.C. all the time."

"The protestors are saying that either polling is broken or the elections are broken. Which do you think it is?"

"It could be either. Maybe *polling is broken*. Maybe *the elections are broken*. Probably there will be investigations. Probably, eventually, the *truth will out."*

"What is your profession, if I may ask?"

"I'm a poly sci university professor," he replied.

"Do you sympathize with the protestors?" asked Monica.

"I'm just an observer, really," said Ray. "I probably shouldn't say this, but I don't even vote."

"You're a poly sci professor, and you don't vote?" asked Monica, amazed.

Ray smiled. "No, I just study politics. It's like being an ornithologist. To watch birds, you don't have to lay eggs."

"Don't you think votes matter?" asked Monica.

"Well, *you know what Stalin said: it's not who votes that counts. It's who counts the votes."*

"So, our elections aren't fair and accurate?" asked Monica.

"Well, *no one on either side of the aisle has ever been serious about election integrity*. If they were, there would be an election day, not a month, and America would count ballots by hand in one evening like they do in France."

"But even so," said Monica, "isn't it a disgrace to swarm the Capitol and break into the building? It's against the law."

"Well, what is it Jesus said about the Jerusalem Temple? *'There will not be left here one stone upon another that will not be thrown down.'* And what did Cicero say? *'The more laws, the less justice.'*"

"Are you advocating that?"

"No," said Ray. *"But in the history of the world, these things happen."*

"Do you think all this portends a new American Civil War?"

"A new Civil War? I don't know. Not like the first one, probably, but *there could be one;* I guess we'll see."

"Can I get your name?" asked Monica.

"Ray Almaviva," said Ray. "But I'd rather you didn't quote me on all of this."

"I hear you," said Monica, noncommittally. And the camera stopped rolling.

CHAPTER 3

THE DISCOVERY

Ilsa walked along the streets of Washington, D.C., towards the National Archives. She passed a magazine stand where the late afternoon newspapers had huge headlines blaring "PROFESSOR ALMAVIVA—FOMENTS—INSURRECTION." Brooding, however, on her interview with Dr. Dr. Bradford, she hurried by without noticing. But she could not help feeling that the whole town was fraught, if fraught was the word she wanted, with anxiety. Even though she hadn't been there, she sensed that the events at the Capitol had left everyone on edge. There were fewer than normal people on the streets, although there were frightening little mobs of tough kids prowling about, seeking whom they might devour.

As she turned down Eleventh Street NW, one of these gangs suddenly came running along the street and began throwing bricks into the front window of a trendy apparel shop. They stormed the store and began to make off with armloads of expensive garments and handbags. Ilsa stopped in her tracks, stunned. Recovering from her shock, she thought, "I could call the police." She took out her cell phone and began to dial, when one of the gangsters, an overweight tough guy with braided hair, rolled up to Ilsa with a snarl.

"Put down the phone, sister," he said.

A second gangster, this time a slender female with blond dreadlocks and a nose ring, knocked the phone out of Ilsa's hands. "No need for cops," she said.

A third gangster, a very short kid with no hair and sagging pants, shouted, "We're peaceful protesters!"

And then they ran away with their loot, disappearing around the corner of the block with armfuls of garments flapping in the breeze. Ilsa stooped to pick up her phone. "They didn't look like peaceful protesters," she thought.

Recovering her aplomb, the determined scholar continued to the National Archives, where she presented her university credentials to a moth-eaten employee. He led her down a back staircase into a large, unlit room. The employee snapped on the lights, which fizzed and popped slightly before coming on. The room was filled with stacks of moldering documents. A mouse scurried into a dark corner.

"You can look around for a couple of hours," said the employee, "but you can't remove anything without special permission."

"Of course," said Ilsa.

The employee beetled out, letting the door creak shut behind him. Ilsa found herself spookily alone in a room full of decaying and often uncategorized documents, all from the Revolutionary War. One might think that documents from the Revolutionary War all had been classified, but masses of them, in fact, had not been, because, as Ilsa knew too well, scholars seldom do original research. They mostly just cite and recycle each other's theses.

"Now, what am I looking for?" she asked herself, aloud. She often spoke to herself. And answered, too. It made her feel less alone. "Something unusual," she continued, "Something surprising. But how do I find it?" The only thing to do was just start leafing through all this stuff.

Ilsa went over to one of the stacks and began opening files and turning pages. She found many curious documents and many dull ones. Still, nothing really suggested a line of inquiry until finally, she found an ancient parchment with the superscript "Title Deed to the Duchy of Almaviva."

"Have you ever heard of the Duchy of Almaviva?" she asked herself. "Never," she replied. She read down the lines of a beautifully handwritten script. Then she came to signatures on the bottom: "Benjamin Franklin, John Adams, James Madison, John Hancock, Thomas Jefferson, Samuel Chase."

"Are they real?" she asked herself. "Well," she answered, "I'm going to research this and find out." Ilsa took a photo of the ancient document with her phone. Then she stood up and said eagerly to herself, "To the internet!"

She snapped out the crackling lights in the haunted room and let the door whine shut eerily behind her.

CHAPTER 4

THE
IDENTIFICATION

Back in her study, the first thing Ilsa did was consult her database of genealogical records. The first Duke of Almaviva had the extraordinary name of Don Raimondo de Borbón y Cortés Almaviva. Apparently, he died in Austria in 1805, fighting on Napoleon's side at the Battle of Austerlitz. The family tree, however, branched out to America, but then gave out with one of the Duke's descendants, who was an orphan. The orphanage where he was raised burned down in the twentieth century, and all the records, being paper in those days, perished in the fire. But Ilsa was determined. She knew how history works. Everyone leaves traces, even if they try not to.

So, she began consulting the records of living people with the surname Almaviva. The name was ranked the 419,766th most popular name in America, so the estimated population of people in America named Almaviva was zero, and the proportion per

100,000 Americans named Almaviva was also zero. That was the statistical analysis, which might have been discouraging, but for the fact that Ilsa, doggedly persisting in her queries, did discover one human being with that name: Ray Almaviva, a resident and fellow professor in Washington, D.C. A thrill shot through Ilsa's veins. This had to be her man. She already could feel her thesis burgeoning in her mind and bearing fabulous fruit, like the Tree of Life blooming in the New Jerusalem. Tenure was in view!

As a skilled researcher, it was with Ilsa the work of mere moments to track Ray Almaviva down to his lair. She took a cab across town to the other university. Then standing before the door of Ray's university office, she took a deep breath and knocked.

"Door's open," called Ray in a bored tone.

Ilsa ventured in, clutching a bulging file under her arm. The deep breath she had taken on the other side of the door was, at the sight of Ray, taken away. He was gorgeous! She had expected an elderly pedant with a shock of white hair like Geppetto in *Pinocchio*. But this man's Antonio Banderas charm seemed to reach across the room, crush her in his arms, and shower burning kisses upon her upturned lips. She shivered and tried to shake the sensation off. "To business," she told herself.

Ray looked up and scanned Ilsa from North to South and then from East to West. It only took a moment. Ray was in love. Again. Probably. Conscious of his dashing Hispanic allure, Ray was always optimistic about his chances with the female sex. He had left a very long string of girlfriends in his wake, but there was something about this woman, who projected such shyness about her untapped feminine charms, that made his already active pulse race. Somehow he couldn't help imagining her blundering into his bedroom at midnight wearing nothing but a towel. Those many affairs of yore, he told himself, were just steppingstones of his dead past on which he was rising to the discovery of his one, true love. And here she was. Probably.

Ilsa shivered. She thought she wasn't clever and beautiful enough for a man like Ray, but she told herself, you never can tell.

"Have you got a minute?" she asked, after finding her voice.

"I've got hours. How about dinner tonight?" asked Ray.

Ilsa shifted nervously.

"Do you mind if I sit down?" she asked.

"Of course," said Ray, "make yourself comfortable."

Ilsa sat in one of the two chairs in front of Ray's desk. "I have a problem," she confided.

Ray frowned. "Don't tell me you have a fiancé?"

Goose bumps rippled across Ilsa's skin.

"No," she replied. "It's not that. I have to publish a thesis."

Ray was pleasantly relieved. "Publish or perish, eh?" he asked, smiling.

"Exactly," said Ilsa.

"Got an idea?" he asked.

"I think I do," said she.

"How can I help?" asked Ray.

"Well, can I ask you about your family tree?"

Ray shifted in his seat and grinned. "Wait—am I the subject of your thesis?"

"You might be," said Ilsa.

"Well, then you definitely have to let me take you to dinner," said Ray.

Ilsa flushed a deep crimson. "Can you tell me about your paternal grandfather?"

Ray laughed. "What do you want to know?"

"What can you tell me?"

"Well," said Ray, "he was a wonderful old guy. Gentle, kind, loved children, and children loved him."

"What were his parents like?" asked Ilsa.

"He didn't have any," said Ray. "Well, he must have had some at some point, of course. But he was an orphan."

Ilsa's heart danced a fandango. She peeked into her file, shivered, and pressed on. "Did his parents die when he was young?" she asked.

"Nobody knows," said Ray. "The orphanage where he was raised burned to the ground years ago. Back in those days, a person's records were all paper, you know, and they perished in the fire. So, my family tree before Grandad kind of blows a fuse."

Ilsa sat in silence, staring at Ray for a long, expectant minute.

"I know who you are," she said at last.

"So do I," said Ray.

"No, you don't."

"Let me get this straight," said Ray, bristling slightly. "You know who I am, but I don't know who I am."

"That's right."

"So, who am I?"

But just then, an alarm sounded on his computer. He shook himself free of her glittering eye and said, "I've got class in ten minutes. But you interest me strangely. How about we meet for dinner, and you can explain?"

"OK," surrendered Ilsa.

Ray stood up. Ilsa stood up.

"Meet me at Union Station at six o'clock this evening," said Ray. "Do you like Ethiopian food?" Before she could answer, Ray said, "Good," wrapping things up. And off he biffed.

CHAPTER 5

A DATE
WITH DESTINY

Ilsa arrived at Union Station at a quarter to six. That landmark has a large and beautiful edifice. Ilsa gazed at the marble inscription: "It is in traveling a man must carry knowledge with him if he would bring home knowledge." She had never thought of that. She had hardly traveled anywhere. Maybe if she traveled, she would be more like Ray: confident, a winner, a tenured, popular professor. Oh, he was living a life to remember.

Then she began to wonder if he had remembered after all. She glanced at her watch. Six o'clock. Where was he? Then she began to doubt her memory. Had he said the main entrance or somewhere else? Had he said Union Station, come to that? Suddenly, Ray materialized behind her and chirped, "Hello!"

Ilsa made a vertical leap like a springbok on the Serengeti plain.

"Sorry," said Ray. "Didn't mean to startle you."

Ilsa floated gently back to earth.

"Let's go for dinner," Ray suggested. "I think you'll find the *ti'hilo* delicious."

"*Ti'hilo?*" asked Ilsa.

"It's like Ethiopian fondue. Barley balls pierced by wooden forks and dipped in a piquant sauce made from pulses, flour, and spices. Had it before?"

"It's been a while," bluffed Ilsa.

Stirring cups of coffee after their meal in Ray's upscale Ethiopian bistro, Ray smiled, and asked, "So, how was your day?"

Ilsa sighed. "It wasn't ideal."

"What happened?"

Ilsa recounted the dreadful interview with Dr. Dr. Bradford M. Bradford. Ray patted her hand. She shivered, and Ray also felt the unspoken thrill.

"That's not much of a problem," he said. "Just research something and publish it. I do it all the time. Something will come up. You said something did, didn't you? Namely, me?"

"Yes," she said, "well, what you told me about your grandfather fits my research." She pulled the bulging file from her purse and laid it on the table. "You have an unusual last name."

"That's true," said Ray. "I've never met anyone else named Almaviva."

"You wouldn't have. You're the only one."

"Really?"

"The only one in America. It's exciting," said Ilsa, breathlessly.

"Well, not that exciting," said Ray.

"More than you think," said Ilsa mysteriously. "Have you ever heard of Don Raimondo de Borbón y Cortés Almaviva?"

"Never."

"Well, he was your ancestor. I did more research this afternoon, and the identification is absolute."

"OK, who was he?"

"Governor of the Spanish Caribbean colony of Santa Cecilia. But he came to America during the Revolutionary War and then went to France with the Marquis de Lafayette to push for revolution there. He died in Austria, fighting on Napoleon's side at the Battle of Austerlitz."

"Austerlitz?" asked Ray.

"Yes," said Ilsa. "After an unfortunate encounter with a Russian cannon."

"And he's my ancestor?" asked Ray.

"Without a doubt. Look at this," she said. She took out her smartphone and showed Ray the image of a yellowed parchment. The ornate, calligraphic letters at the top spelled "Title Deed to the Duchy of Almaviva."

"What's that?" asked he.

"Your inheritance," she said. "And look at the signatures on the bottom."

Ray pinched the image to enlarge it and read: "Benjamin Franklin, John Adams, James Madison, John Hancock, Thomas Jefferson, Samuel Chase."

"Are they real?" asked Ray.

"I'm pretty sure they are," said Ilsa.

"What does it mean?" he asked.

"I don't really know yet, but I think it means you're important," she whispered darkly.

The waiter came and dropped the check on their table. Ray put a credit card on it. The waiter whisked it away, brought back the payment slip, and Ray signed it.

"Let's get some fresh air," he said.

CHAPTER 6

LIGHTNING STRIKES

Ray and Ilsa walked thoughtfully through the chilly evening. Ray had his hands clasped behind his back. He was turning over ideas about how to get Ilsa back to his apartment. Ilsa, regrettably, had gone all business, her brain ticking over. Dark clouds were gathering, and the wind was rising. Ray pulled up his collar. A distant murmur of thunder rolled. Ilsa broke the silence.

"I can prove that you are, in fact, a direct descendant of Don Raimondo de Borbón y Cortés Almaviva," she told Ray.

"Well, that's nice," said Ray, "I have a family tree, after all. But what about your thesis? How is my ancestry going to be your Big Idea? I mean, it's hardly an earth-shattering discovery. Someone had to be the old duffer's descendant."

"Well, isn't it curious?"

A flicker of lightning illuminated a large, dark cloud. Ilsa looked nervously at the gathering storm. Still, the thrill of historical discovery held her in its grip. "What about his having the name of Spain's royal family, de Borbón? And the name of the Conqueror of Mexico, Cortés?"

The thunder rumbled more ominously.

"So, what, I'm royalty?" laughed Ray. "And a conqueror? Come on."

"Don't you see?" asked Ilsa. "He was *somebody*. The ancestry records I found prove he's your ancestor, and he was *somebody*. So, maybe you're somebody, too. Now the question is, who? What was he all about? And what are you all about?"

A lightning bolt flickered. Large raindrops began to splatter on the ground.

"Come on," said Ray. "We'd better duck inside somewhere before we're soaked."

Just then, six black SUVs roared up and surrounded Ray and Ilsa, blue lights flashing. Out of them jumped heavily armed FBI agents in body armor. The Special Agent in Charge, who happened to be the same brawny man who had been wearing the red cap at the Capitol, spoke through a bullhorn. "FBI: Special Agent in Charge Schweppes. Put your hands behind your heads. You're under arrest."

Suddenly, a spiral of lightning snaked across the frowning sky and struck Ray and Ilsa. In a spectacular flash, they vanished. An earth-shattering bang of thunder knocked over all the FBI agents. Ilsa's file of genealogical records flew into the air. The thoroughly singed pages fluttered down the street, twisting in the frantic breeze. The bullhorn fell from Agent Schweppes' limp fingers. The rain began to fall like bullets.

Part Two

Happy the man, and happy he alone,
He who can call today his own,
He who, secure within, can say,
Tomorrow do your worst, for I have lived today.

–Horace

CHAPTER 7

SANTA CECILIA

The tropical sun flickered between the swaying fronds of palm trees overhead. Ray and Ilsa rubbed their necks and blinked as they came out of their stupor. Their hair stood on end in frazzled locks, like quills upon the fretful porcupine. Their clothes were scorched, but they were alive. Or were they? Speechless, they gazed at their surroundings. Above them was an azure sky with fluffy clouds shaped like Spanish galleons sailing across a celestial sea. Birds chattered and sang in the foliage, which was fragrant and brilliant with blue, and pink and yellow flowers. Had they died? Was this heaven? Or, perish the thought, since obviously they were in the tropics, the other place?

From nearby came gentle singing. They staggered to their feet and walked to a hedge and peered over. There they saw a marketplace square where men were setting up stalls to sell their wares. As they worked the merchants sang a catchy, Caribbean tune.

SONG: *SANTA CECILIA*

Morning is breaking,
our city is waking,

Pretty *señoritas*
soon will catch every eye.
We bring bananas,
scarves and bandannas,
and coral-colored fish
for all the ladies to buy.

As the merchants set out their wares, the hoped-for pretty *señoritas* began to drift into the plaza, consciously swaying their hips so that their floral skirts whirled around their shapely legs. They sang a nonchalant song as they wandered seductively through the market.

How sweet the breeze that brings
the flowers' perfume and
makes the palm trees sway!
How sweet to greet all those
We meet along our way!
And when the stars
come out and bathe our dreams
in silver streams
from far above,
and the guitars
make every head to turn
and heart to yearn for love,
Then we will sing and play,
and seize the day,
and dance the hours away.
For if tomorrow
brings us sorrow,
who can say?

The ladies turned to the business of shopping, which consisted largely of tsk-tsking insultingly over the merchants' wares in a ploy meant to drive their prices down. They sang with theatrical scorn.

Your mangoes are bruised.
This shawl appears used.
We're frankly amused
You expect us to buy.
Your fishes are old,
Your cornbread has mold,
And all of your prices are too high.

Used to the ladies' rituals, the merchants, like plaintive troubadours, replied in song.

Oh, ladies, do not jest,
we do our best,
You know it's true.
Everything is fresh,
especially for you.
And if you say
the prices that we ask you pay
Are just a little high,
Don't run away!
We'll always find a way
to satisfy.
And if you *señoritas*
Care to meet us
Later on,
Beneath a starry sky
We'll dream and sigh
'til dawn.

Captivated more by flirting than commerce, all the men and women in the marketplace joined together, dancing picturesquely as they sang.

> Santa Cecilia
> We'll always feel ya,
> Here in our hearts,
> Our sweet island home.
> Your sons and daughters
> Over the waters
> Far from your hills
> shall never roam.

From the fort's parapets on the hilltop, a lookout gazed beyond the palm fronds that rippled over the sparkling sea. "A sail! A sail!" he cried.

"Ours?" shouted one of the merchants, alarmed.

"Or English pirates?" asked one of the ladies, anxiously.

The Governor, Don Raimondo de Borbón y Cortés Almaviva, splendidly attired, appeared on the fort's parapet. He goggled through a spyglass at a forest of billowing sails offshore.

"The Treasure Fleet," he said to his faithful aide-de-camp, Feliz. The fleet was sailing from Peru to Cádiz, bearing its annual harvest of silver and gold. It was calling at Santa Cecilia to re-victual before crossing the broad Atlantic.

"Ours!" cried the lookout to the people in the plaza below. A cheer echoed back.

"Fire a salute to the Admiral, Feliz," ordered Don Raimondo.

"*Sí, Señor.*" Feliz cupped his hands and shouted to the soldiers on the parapet, "Fire of the guns!"

The people in the marketplace below were thrilled at the prospect of sailors from the fleet coming ashore with their purses filled from their last port of call in Panama. They sang with joy.

> This time of year
> We love to hear
> The mighty cannons roar!

A boom from the parapet rolled out to sea as the great cannons spoke. The folk continued to sing.

> They fire to greet
> The Treasure Fleet
> Come here once more.

> From Potosí
> It brings the gold
> That old King Carlos craves,
> Defying pirates, storms, and reefs
> And crashing waves.

> And when the sailors spy
> Santa Cecilia's
> Hills and palms and gleaming shore,
> They raise a cry...

In the distance, the cheers of incoming sailors rang out, delighting the people in the plaza, who continued to sing.

> To come explore
> our paradise once more.

Briskly, the merchants replaced all their usual price placards with higher-priced placards. They sang with glee.

> And in a trice,
> We nicely raise the price
> of everything.
> So they spend here
> The gleaming gold
> Meant for the King.

Sailors leaped from the fleet's lighters onto the quay. Their officers tried to keep them together with their revictualing parties, but they scattered everywhere, buying food and drink and flirting with the girls. The island men serenaded the sailors.

> Welcome, you sailors,
> Bring all your wages,
> Drink to the King
> Before you sail for Spain.

The women crooned alluringly to the mariners.

> Let wine and beauty
> Lighten your duty.
> Who knows if you'll ever
> Put ashore here again?

The *señoritas* danced with the sailors. Their officers and the marines tried to stop them but soon gave up and joined in dancing with the girls themselves. The people of Santa Cecilia and the officers and sailors of the Spanish fleet all raised their voices in happy song.

> How sweet the breeze that brings
> the flowers' perfume and
> makes the palm trees sway!

How sweet to please all those
We meet along our way!
And when the stars
come out and bathe our dreams
in silver streams
from far above,
and the guitars
make every head to turn
and heart to yearn for love,
We sing and play,
and seize the day,
and dance the hours away.
For if tomorrow
brings us sorrow,
who can say?
Now come, let's seize the day!

The song ended in a beautiful tableau. Then the sailors sat on benches and ordered rum or shopped in the market or mingled with the locals. Ray and Ilsa gazed at each other, entranced.

"Where are we?" asked Ray.

"Santa Cecilia," said Feliz, who had come up noiselessly behind them.

Ray and Ilsa leaped in the air like rockets. When they recovered from their surprise, they turned to Feliz and asked, "Who are you?"

"I am the righthand man of the Governor."

Ray and Ilsa looked at each other again, open-mouthed. Ray found his voice first. "Where did you say we are?"

Feliz made a quizzical expression. "Santa Cecilia," he said. "The island colony of His Majesty King Carlos III of Spain."

"You mean the colony," said Ilsa, "governed by His Excellency

Don Raimondo de Borbón y Cortés, Count of Almaviva?"

"Yes," said Feliz. "You know His Excellency?"

With mounting excitement, Ilsa said, "This man is a Ray Almaviva, a relative of the Count."

Feliz squinted in disbelief.

"It's true," said Ilsa. "A distant relative."

"Very distant," said Ray.

"And you are...?" asked Feliz, looking at Ilsa.

"His, um, sister," she said, improvising. She couldn't say colleague or companion. In the Spanish empire of the eighteenth century, people might take that in a compromising way.

"Were you shipwrecked?" asked Feliz, scanning the newcomers' jeans and casual shirts.

"Yes, we were shipwrecked, sort of," said Ray, glowering resentfully at Ilsa.

"*Bueno,*" said Feliz, "come with me to the fort."

As they crossed the market square with Feliz, Ray and Ilsa couldn't help admiring the quaint and brilliantly colorful costumes of the islanders. The place seemed like a dream.

"What day is this?" asked Ray.

"It's Thursday," said Feliz.

"What year?" asked Ilsa, trembling.

Feliz stopped in his tracks and stared suspiciously at the oddly singed strangers. He decided to let the Governor question them further, so he answered simply, "1776."

Ilsa gaped in excitement. She clutched Ray's arm. "Seventeen seventy-six!" she exclaimed.

Ray scowled. "See what you've got me into?"

CHAPTER 8

HIS EXCELLENCY

Don Raimondo welcomed the strangers to the governor's palace with the easy cordiality of a high-born Spanish grandee. When Ray and Ilsa entered his opulent office, he stood respectfully as a lady entered the room, even though she was a lady who looked like she had recently been hit by lightning. The don seated his guests in comfortable chairs near a terrace that commanded a sweeping view of the harbor and the Treasure Fleet riding at anchor beyond the breakwater.

"You are most welcome," said Don Raimondo to Ray. "I was unaware that I had relatives in North America, but Feliz tells me your wife has an uncanny knowledge of our family tree. That is sufficient proof of our consanguinity."

"Not wife," blushed Ilsa. "Sister."

Don Raimondo raised his eyebrows, suspecting something was not quite on the level. He had read Genesis and was aware of Abraham's sly habit of fobbing off his wife Sarah as his sister. But he was too courteous to probe further into the particulars of their relationship. He could not, however, forbear to remark on their attire.

"These costumes of yours," he said, noting their jeans. "Is this what they are wearing these days in North America?"

"They were when we left," said Ray.

"Very revolutionary. With your permission, I will arrange for you to have a fresh change of clothes."

"That would be wonderful," said Ilsa.

With a snap of his fingers, Don Raimondo summoned Feliz, who, having heard the order, was already scurrying into action.

"I would be most interested," said Don Raimondo, "to hear news of the political situation in North America right now."

"It's terrible," said Ray.

"By right now," whispered Ilsa to Ray, "he means in the year 1776."

"Ah," said Ray. "Well, you're the historian. You tell him."

"It's terrible," said Ilsa.

"But how?" asked Don Raimondo.

"The Continental Congress is just a talking shop," said Ilsa. "They don't appropriate any money or supplies. George Washington's army has to fight without arms, or ammunition, or shoes. The British left Boston all right, but they took New York. And they're threatening Philadelphia. Most people don't believe the Continentals can win."

"Although they will in the end, of course," said Ray.

"Ah," said Don Raimondo, "an optimist. Like me. A true Almaviva."

Ray smiled wanly.

"I have invited our wealthiest planters to dinner tonight to host the Admiral of the fleet," said Don Raimondo. "I would be honored if you would join us."

"The honor," said Ilsa, "would be all ours."

Feliz led them to their quarters. Once inside their room, Ray hissed to Ilsa, "Let me tell you, sister, this is the worst date I've ever been on."

"Is this a date?" asked Ilsa.

"It was supposed to be," said Ray. "But I ask you out, and the next thing I know, I wake up two hundred and forty-four years ago."

"Well, I am so sorry to disappoint you," said Ilsa, frostily. "I find it all rather fun."

"Oh, you do, do you?" asked Ray.

"Yes, I do," said Ilsa.

Ray dearly wanted to make a satirical reply to this, but at the moment, when he really needed something snappy to say, nothing came to mind. What did the French call it? Ah, yes, *l'esprit de l'escalier*, the spirit of the staircase. It's when you think of what you wish you would have said only when you're standing on the staircase outside the room where, a moment ago, you should have said it. The best he could do was to impose on Ilsa a frozen silence.

CHAPTER 9

A CUNNING PLAN

That evening in the governor's mansion, Don Raimondo concluded dinner with a toast to His Majesty, King Carlos of Spain. The Admiral and the conclave of bored, wealthy planters staggered drunkenly to their feet and raised their glasses. Ray and Ilsa, now dressed in outfits of the period and a trifle tipsy on the excellent wine, did the same. "The King!" they all declared in chorus. The Admiral raised his glass and proposed another toast.

"To His Excellency, our host, the Governor of His Majesty's Crown Colony of Santa Cecilia!"

"The Governor!" cried one and all.

Don Raimondo proposed a final toast. "To the Admiral of the Treasure Fleet, which brings Peru's silver and gold to Spain!"

"The Admiral!" they chorused. Ray, who was drinking a little too much and trying to forget, slipped and spilled a bit of wine on the Admiral's sleeve of Mechlin lace. The fastidious officer scowled and scrubbed his immaculate cuff.

After these exertions, the guests all resumed their seats, and Don Raimondo dismissed the servants. Closing the door himself, he wheeled dramatically and fixed his guests with a piercing gaze. Too much wealth, too much wine, and too little to do, he thought. They were a lazy bunch. He could but try to arouse their imperial zeal.

"*Señores*, I'm sure you have all read the gazettes from Madrid."

They glanced at each other. Well, of course they hadn't. What would be the use of that?

"If you have," continued the Governor, "You know that the world is changing. I do not wish in any way to disparage the majesty of my dear cousin, King Carlos III, but it is time for plain speaking. *Señores*, Spain is the doddering, old man of Europe!"

The dons shifted uncomfortably. They, like everyone else, knew that this was true. But saying it openly was detestable form.

"You are aware of what is happening in the British Colonies up north?"

"We have heard rumors," said one of the dons, tentatively.

"Rumors that our Most Catholic Majesty is supporting the rebels," said another.

"But in secret," said a third.

"And why in secret?" challenged Don Raimondo. "Louis XVI of France is supporting them in secret. Secrecy is beneath the honor of Spain! We should repay Jorge III for all the humiliations England has given to Spain in the New World! Our world! I tell you, *Señores*, now is the time for us to make a difference and tip the scales."

"Us?" asked the Admiral, boggled.

"Us!" thundered Don Raimondo. "Open action. Show that decrepit madman of Hanover that he is up against the whole Empire of Spain!"

"What exactly does Your Excellency have in mind?" asked one don, warily.

"Funds," said Don Raimondo. That single word, funds, slithered painfully through the assembly of wealthy planters like Herod's worm.

"I want to collect a tribute for the American rebels. It's clearly in Spain's interest to do so."

The dons contemplated the port gravely. None of them felt it could be in their interest to do so. At last, a second don ventured: "I think, Your Excellency, we would all agree that England's defeat would be our gain."

"Good," beamed Don Raimondo.

"And it's not a question of money," said a don.

"Ah, please don't say that," shuddered the Governor. "When anyone tells me that it is not a question of money, I always know that it is nothing but."

"Your Excellency," reasoned another don. "I think the issue is this...Rights of Man nonsense."

"Nonsense?" gasped Don Raimondo. "Is not their Declaration of Independence inspired?"

"Inspired, yes," said a don. "Prudent, no. How would it play among our plantation laborers?"

"This agitation is a good way to fan an uprising," murmured another don, decanting more port. The room trembled with a murmur of assent.

"And if the colonials up north prevail," said a don, "the next thing you know, Mexico and Peru would cut ties with Madrid. It wouldn't be worth hanging on to a little patch like Santa Cecilia then."

"We'd all go packing home to Galicia or Estremadura as plucked as a roast chicken," said another don.

"Better stay out of the whole show, Excellency," said a don.

"Watch and wait," said another don.

"By far the soundest policy," said a don.

"You reject my plan?" asked Don Raimondo.

The dons stared at His Excellency, unblinking. He was cousin to the King. He embodied royal authority on Santa Cecilia. But he was espousing a policy radically beyond anything the Escorial had ever sanctioned. It was a sticky business. One might lose one's head either way.

Realizing that his plea had fallen on deaf ears, Don Raimondo flung defiance in their teeth. "I fling," he said grandly, "defiance in your teeth."

They looked back and forth across the table, unsure what, under such circumstances, etiquette now required. But Don Raimondo drew himself to a dignified height as a signal that the reception was over. Relieved, the dons rose, and the Admiral rose with them. The dons thanked the Governor and filed nervously out.

"I hope," said the Admiral, pausing before the door, "that Your Excellency will allow me to return tonight's compliment by hosting you aboard my flagship for dinner tomorrow evening. I have," he chortled greedily, "an excellent chef."

Don Raimondo stiffly nodded his assent, and the Admiral departed. Only Ray, Ilsa, and Feliz remained. The Governor, agitated, stalked out onto the terrace. The soft, Caribbean breeze caressed their cheeks. Ray tried but failed to suppress a gentle hiccup. Don Raimondo paced, watching the moon scatter silver dollars across the undulating surface of the sea. Then he stopped and faced Ray and Ilsa.

"Cousins, there comes a time when a man must take a chance. A gamble to change the world for the better. I have a cunning plan. A risky one. But a very big idea. Will you join me?"

"A Big Idea? Yes, yes!" said Ilsa. "That's just what I need."

"Spoken with the fearless nonchalance of a true Almaviva," said Don Raimondo. He took her hand gallantly and kissed it. "So beautiful," he said, "and yet so bold."

Ray scowled. The wine had fogged his perceptions, perhaps, but as much of a thorn in his side as Ilsa had proven to be, there was something about the Count of Almaviva lushing her up like this that irked him.

Don Raimondo put his arm around Ilsa's waist and led her to the terrace. Gazing at the North Star, he murmured a vow.

"General Washington, you will not fight your revolution alone!"

Ilsa gazed at this valiant cavalier and sighed. Ray gently hiccupped again.

CHAPTER 10

THE TREASURE

The next day, as thunderheads swept across the powder-blue sky, the Governor, Ray, Ilsa, Feliz, and a few trusted soldiers and servants, sailed out among the ships of the Treasure Fleet, which rode proudly at anchor in the gentle swells. Ray's jaws were set tensely; his complexion was pale with seasickness. Ilsa's cheeks, by contrast, were blooming. Her hair, loosed, was streaming behind her in the breeze. Don Raimondo, believing she was his cousin, watched her out of the tail of his eye with approval. Bold girl! His own mother had been like that.

All around the Governor's pinnacle, a fleet of barges, low in the waves, dragged under billowing sails, bringing water and stores to the ships from shore. In the stern sheets of his craft, Don Raimondo carried a gift of several barrels of amontillado. He knew his man. This admiral was as greedy a gourmand as ever surrounded a veal chop. The amontillado would put him off his guard. The Governor's pinnacle tacked into the wind until the sail luffed, and it slid neatly alongside the flagship, *Infanta de Castille.*

"Reef sail!" cried Feliz.

The crew smartly gathered canvas and plunged their oars into the waves, casting a veil of clean, Caribbean spray over the Governor and his company. The *Infanta's* crew lowered a cradle to haul Don Raimondo up, but disdaining this convenience for gouty old captains, he scrambled up the rope ladder like a midshipman and bounded athletically aboard. Turning to Ilsa, the Count extended a gallant hand and helped her up. Eyeing the rope ladder dubiously, Ray hesitated.

"After you, *Señor*," said Feliz.

"Yes, of course," said Ray, and seizing the rope ladder, he hauled himself up awkwardly. Feliz and the rest of Don Raimondo's team followed. The bosun piped them aboard, and the Admiral, the ship's Captain, and all the officers smartly saluted the cousin of their King. When the bosun had finished shrilling, the first officer proclaimed: "His Excellency, Don Raimondo de Borbón y Cortés, Count of Almaviva and Governor of His Most Catholic Majesty's colony, Santa Cecilia."

The Admiral bowed, his fat girth creasing. "Your Excellency!"

Don Raimondo inclined with the scornful pride of a hidalgo whose veins coursed Bourbon blood. "Admiral, may I present my cousins, Ray and Ilsa Almaviva?"

The Admiral bowed politely, saying, "Enchanted to see you again. You are most welcome to my ship."

Ilsa curtseyed, her lovely floral skirt of the period swirling. Ray bowed stiffly. He wasn't quite sure how you're supposed to do it.

"My ship is at your command, Your Excellency," said the Admiral.

Don Raimondo sniped a glance at his picked men, whose shifty eyes were sweeping the deck. "At my command," he repeated dreamily. *"Bueno.* Then please be good enough to take the *Infanta* to sea."

The Admiral was stunned. "I beg your pardon?"

"Put to sea," repeated the Governor, casually inspecting his nails.

"To sea?" asked the Admiral.

"To sea," said Don Raimondo.

The Admiral looked like a man who hadn't known it was loaded. "But Your Excellency...we just got here!"

Don Raimondo took the Admiral to one side. "These are troubling times, my good man. I am not here only to accept your invitation to dinner. I have something to say to you of the utmost delicacy. It can only be said in total secrecy if we put to sea."

The Admiral boggled.

"Your Excellency, we have complete privacy in my cabin...."

"Not," said Don Raimondo, "enough privacy for what I have to impart. Now, Admiral, have you fully seized my order, and are you prepared to obey it, or are you, too, infected by the revolutionary sentiments that are, in this hemisphere, just now rather rife?"

"No, Your Excellency! I would give my life for the blood royal."

"Let us hope it doesn't come to that. Now put to sea."

The Admiral turned to his Captain helplessly. "Captain, prepare to sail...!" Then he turned back to Don Raimondo. "What course, Excellency?"

"North-northeast."

The Captain turned to his First Lieutenant. "Signal the fleet. Weigh anchor. Course: north by northeast."

"Not the fleet," interrupted Don Raimondo. "Just the flagship."

"What!" exclaimed the Admiral. "That is impossible!"

Don Raimondo shot him a severe, punishable-by-death sort of look. The Admiral extended his pudgy hands in despair.

"Your Excellency, we cannot put the *Infanta* to sea without her escorts." He took the Governor aside, whispering hoarsely. "The Peruvian gold is in her hold. All the other ships carry only silver. The *Infanta* must be protected."

A mirthless smile flickered across Don Raimondo's supple lips. "Are you questioning my judgment?"

"It's not that, but..."

"I am sure," said the Count with a meaningful nod at the Captain, "that this officer would be happy, if necessary, to assume your command."

The Captain cleared his throat.

"No, Your Excellency. I mean, yes, Your Excellency."

The Admiral drew himself up and turned to his second-in-command. Sighing, he said, "Just the *Infanta*, Captain, not the fleet."

The Captain exchanged scandalized glances with his officers, but he said: "Signal the fleet, Lieutenant. They stay put. Weigh anchor. Put the *Infanta* to sea, north by northeast."

As the *Infanta's* crew labored at the capstan, drawing up the twin ten-thousand-pound bowers anchors, there was a good deal of signaling around the fleet. The captains of the frigates peered suspiciously at the flagship. Were these false flags? But, no, they were in Spanish waters with no enemy in sight, and the orders from the Admiral's mast were plain as day. In a little over an hour, they watched the *Infanta's* reach the blue horizon. In a few more moments, her royal sails sank below it, and she was out of sight.

"How about that dinner, then?" said Don Raimondo cheerfully.

Deflated, the Admiral led the way to his dining quarters in the aft section of the upper gun deck. Don Raimondo suppressed a smile. Few of the grandees of Seville could have rivaled the lavishness of the Admiral's table, even if, rather than gently rolling at anchor, it was now pitching and yawing on the open sea. It amused him to think of the rugged deprivation to which the course of history would soon subject this naval paragon.

Don Raimondo had grand plans. Had it not been for that thought, dinner with the Admiral would have been tedious. The Admiral was a bit of a swine in his cups, and his conversation was clichéd. His main theme consisted of rubbishing the French. Don Raimondo passed the time by conjuring up visions of this commander, adrift for weeks, short of water and food, sunburned and caked with salt, getting picked up by a fishing smack off Havana. Nothing fires the imagination, Don Raimondo reflected, like the deserved suffering of others.

Dinner was not tedious for Ilsa. She was inspecting every detail of attire worn by everyone on board. She was examining the food and how it was prepared. This was a historian's dream, traveling back in time and witnessing history first-hand. Ray was too seasick to care.

When, after the repast, the Admiral began circulating the prized amontillado, the Governor gave a sudden, sharp signal to his men. It was with them the work of a moment to disarm the officers of the flagship. The officers were, in the first place, stunned by the element of surprise. In the second place, the Spanish Navy wasn't what it was in the good old village-incinerating days of Cortés.

Ray instantly forgot his seasickness. He stood up, mouth agape. Don Raimondo had concealed his precise plans from Ray and Ilsa. Ilsa stared with even more astonishment than was usual in her wide eyes. She could not have hoped for more. This was an actual mutiny! A conspiracy! One of those things or both. If writing this up did not get her tenure, nothing would.

Don Raimondo smirked. The ship was his. The Admiral vented a great deal of spluttering outrage, which forced the Count to have him bound and gagged. Winking at Ray and Ilsa, he shouted orders to his men, who hauled the Admiral and the Captain up onto the main deck. Ascending the poop deck, the Count addressed the *Infanta's* crew. He informed them that he had seized the flagship and that he would explain his purpose, but not until every one of the officers and crew declared either for or against him. The men were, of course, torn. Declaring against the Admiral was mutiny, a cut-and-dry hanging offense. But Don Raimondo was the representative of the Crown.

"If you declare for me," announced Don Raimondo, "you will by no means be tried, sentenced, and hung. I cannot give you the details quite yet, but you may rest assured. On my honor."

This changed things. Don Raimondo had pledged upon his honor.

"If you are with me, step to starboard. If not, step to port."

The entire crew stepped to starboard, causing the ship to list. All the officers stepped to port.

"Very good," said Don Raimondo. "Feliz, execute the plan."

"Come on," said Feliz to Ray. Ray had no idea what the plan was, but he followed Feliz in a daze. Ilsa, though neither called nor chosen, tagged eagerly along. Don Raimondo's company escorted the *Infanta's* officers to their quarters and allowed them to select their most precious possessions, but in no case more than what would fit into a biscuit tin. The officers grumbled and swore until Feliz, his gold tooth gleaming, cocked a pistol and held it to the Captain's temple. "Give my compliments to your officers and request that they speak with due courtesy, thus obviating the necessity of my blowing out your brains," he said. Ray gasped. Ilsa stared, half appalled, half enthralled.

"Shut up, you men!" yelled the Captain. They did shut up.

When the officers had gathered their belongings, a grandfather's watch, a cameo of a loved one or of a wife or of both, a compass, a sextant, or a bottle of rum, Feliz marched them back on deck and to the ship's launch, which had rowlocks for sixteen oars. The *Infanta's* officers fit aboard reasonably well. Don Raimondo drew a dagger from a scabbard on his belt, and with elaborate ceremony, cut the line, setting the Admiral and his loyal officers adrift. As the space between the *Infanta* and the launch widened, the maroons cursed the Count with the vivid imagination of sailors.

"You'll hang for this!" ranted the Admiral. "It's piracy!"

Don Raimondo turned calmly to Feliz. "Shoot him," he drawled.

Without turning an eyelash, Feliz drew a pistol from his belt, aimed at the Admiral bobbing about in the launch, and fired. It missed, sending up a spout of seawater over the launch's beam. Ray gulped. Ilsa shrieked, but it was a shriek not of fear but involuntary ecstasy.

"Sorry, sir," said Feliz to Don Raimondo. "I missed."

"Not your time, *Señor!*" Don Raimondo shouted to the Admiral.

"Damn you, *Señor!* Damn you!" seethed the Admiral. And then, the wind going out of him, he bleated plaintively. "But why?"

"Why?" echoed Don Raimondo. "Sir, in the words of Thomas Jefferson, for life, liberty, and the pursuit of happiness!"

"Whose happiness?" moaned the Admiral.

"Mankind's," replied Don Raimondo. "In general," he added. "Not yours in particular." And smiling and waving from the taffrail, he left the empurpled Admiral and his chastened crew in the *Infanta's* shimmering wake.

Don Raimondo mounted the poop deck and faced the crew, who were all standing transfixed on the main deck, gazing up at him. The Count's other men, knowing their place, mingled with the mutineers. Don Raimondo looked over the upturned faces of them all. Beyond them, he could still spy the forlorn launch, whose oars were now stroking rhythmically. Its bow was pointed toward Havana. Clearing his throat, the Count prepared to address his men. He told the crew about the Rights of Man and of aiding the North American colonials. It was a good speech, but the clincher was when the Governor promised to settle them in the new, free colonies of the North, with a share of the King's Peruvian gold from the hold below to help each simple creature on his path. The crew felt, to the last man, that this was yo-heave-ho all around. Deputizing Feliz as his first officer, the Count courteously murmured his wish that the men would return to their posts.

"To your posts, you swabs!" shouted Feliz.

Grinning, the men touched their forelocks and manned their posts. In his teens, Don Raimondo had commanded a ship in the Spanish Navy. Those had been some of the happiest years of his life. He knew his business at sea. Though large, the *Infanta* was a fast ship, and under his competent orders, she sliced through the waves on a brisk north-northeasterly course. When Don Raimondo was sure he had left the fleet's men-o-war safely behind, he gave the order to heave to and sent a sailor on a scaffold over the side. He watched approvingly as the sailor scraped the gilt letters *Infanta de Castille* off the stern. Then he painted over them, in appropriate blood-red, *Derechos de Hombre*, the Rights of Man. When the crew's artist finished the job, Don Raimondo gave an exuberant thumbs up and burst into song.

SONG: *THE RIGHTS OF MAN*

Don Raimondo: Oh, there's a whiff of revolution in the air.
You can't see it, you can't touch it, but it's there.
Every emperor and king
Shudders when he hears us sing
Of freedom's banner flying everywhere.

The crew, bursting with enthusiasm, caught the magic and joined in.

Crew: So, hurrah for the rights of man!
Equality is nature's plan.
We're created to be free,
And we'll never bend a knee,
But fight for that great birthright,
Our noble, global birthright,
Our birthright since the world began.

At Don Raimondo's word, the ship's gunners fired a salute with the cannons. The deafening report rolled over the ocean like thunder.

CHAPTER 11

THE BRITISH BLOCKADE

It was a blustery day off the coast of Virginia, and the rain hammered into the skin like grapeshot. Captain Wesley Biffing of *HMS Prudence* brooded. How had a man with so promising a career ended up on blockade duty outside Chesapeake Bay? New York, fine. Boston, perhaps. But Virginia? Good God, he may as well blockade Savannah. What was the likelihood that any ship worth seizing would stray into a mosquito-infested wasteland like this? Devil take the lucky dogs on the Barbados Station, who at least had a crack at the Spanish Treasure Fleet!

Biffing knew that the only consolation of blockade duty was the chance of seizing an enemy prize ship. A prize ship would make Captain Biffing rich beyond the dreams of Morgan, allowing him to retire from the sea, buy a pleasant estate in Shropshire, hopefully with a title attached, take a seat in the House of Lords, and pass his golden years basking in a reliable stream of bribes from the merchant class of a grateful nation. Biffing leaned on the rail of the poop deck and listened absent-mindedly to the sea chanty of his crew.

SONG: *COUNTRY AND KING*

It's windy and dreary and weary and cold,
Blockading the coast of Virginia.
Life on a frigate so quickly gets old,
Draining out all the spirit within ya.
But it's better to sway
On the ocean all day
Than to march with the infantry far, far away.
So, a salty sea dog
With his tipple of grog
Is content to serve country and King,
O sing:
We'd rather be drenched
Than be shot by the French,
While serving our country and King!

Biffing sang to himself to assuage his own glum feelings.

What hideous luck
To be wretchedly stuck
On this miserable blockading duty!
What I need is a ship
I can capture and strip
To sequester my share of the booty.
Oh, the treasure I'd net
Would settle my debt

And buy an estate with a gold coronet.
Oh, a captain who's wise
Has his eye on the prize
While he's serving his country and King,
O sing
Of a well-deserved rest
In a well-feathered nest
And the riches that duty can bring!

The crew of *HMS Prudence* began a highland hornpipe dance in the sprightly British naval tradition. The first officer, Lieutenant Wilberforce, abandoned himself to the merriment and joined the hijinks of the men. At the end of the dance, they all sang in chorus:

All: Bayoneted impaling
Is much worse than sailing
When serving our country and King,
O sing
How hardtack and weevils
Are just petty evils
When serving our country and King!

Biffing gazed at his nimble crew, wondering how well they would perform in battle. Probably he should put them through their paces sometime. His reverie was splintered, however, like a hammer shattering glass, by the bark of his first officer, Lieutenant Wilberforce. "Sail ho, sir."

The Captain fought back a surge of nausea. How had he been stuck with an idiot like this Canadian dolt Wilberforce as his first officer? Did Nelson have to put up with such dimwits? Of course not. Steeling himself to this insult of fate, he raised his glass to the horizon. Yes, there they were. Royal sails rising out of the distant waves. "What flag?" he enquired, not hopefully.

"What flag?" shrieked Lieutenant Wilberforce to the lookout aloft. His voice always broke like a choir boy's when he shouted commands above the wind whizzing in the rigging. It was intensely annoying to Captain Biffing. The lookout leaned out of the crow's nest and peered to the east. Cupping his hands, he called: "Spain, sir. A Spaniard!"

Lieutenant Wilberforce danced with glee. "Oh, sir! Your prize ship!"

Captain Biffing's upper lip trembled in disdain. "We're not at war with Spain, you imbecile!"

Undeterred, the Lieutenant continued to dance like a dog begging for a biscuit. "But we can take her if she tries to run the blockade, sir."

Captain Biffing's lip froze in mid-sneer. "Really?" He was intrigued. "Give me *The Articles of War.*"

"Aye-aye, sir." Lieutenant Wilberforce dredged up the awful tome, the book of English Admiralty Law that dictated life or death at sea. The Captain thumbed through it feverishly.

"Yes...yes, there it is!"

Biffing's perspective altered. Wilberforce was no longer Wilberforce the human blight. He was Wilberforce, the bearer of glad tidings of great joy, and Captain Biffing marveled that he had for so long overlooked the fine qualities in this young naval officer. He perused the *Articles* again.

"We can, you know," chortled Biffing. "Ha-ha! Yes, we really can!"

"Oh, sir," crooned the Lieutenant. "I am so pleased."

Captain Biffing's glee abruptly congealed. "What are you pleased about?"

"I beg your pardon, sir?"

"This is my prize ship, do you hear? All mine!"

"Aye-aye, sir."

"But I'll recommend your appointment as acting captain when I retire."

"Oh, sir! Thank you, sir."

"And God save the King," mumbled Biffing to himself.

These two sea wolves raised their spyglasses and imbibed their helpless prey.

"Come on, Don Quixote," coaxed the Captain. "Come to Papa!"

From the poop deck of the *Derechos de Hombre*, Don Raimondo watched *HMS Prudence* through his spyglass. Laughing, he handed it to Ray. "Look at this."

Ray struggled with the awkward instrument, until he brought the English ship into view.

"May I see?" asked Ilsa.

"Sure," said Ray sullenly, handing her the glass.

Ilsa trembled at handling a genuine, eighteenth-century telescope and viewing through it an actual eighteenth-century ship. She brought *HMS Prudence* into focus. "Gosh!" she exclaimed.

"May I see?" asked Feliz.

"Yes, yes," said Ilsa, exuberantly.

Feliz pointed the telescope at *HMS Prudence*. His tooth of Incan gold glistened as he grinned.

"Now," said Don Raimondo, clasping his hands together, "we shall see who can fight better, free gentlemen of Spain or lackeys of His Tyrannic Majesty, Jorge III of Great Britain. Battle stations!"

"Battle stations?" asked Ray, alarmed.

"Beat to quarters!" shouted Feliz.

The ship's drummer began to beat a signal with a terrifying rat-a-tat-tat!

"To quarters!" cried Ilsa, quite losing herself to the thrill of it all.

The Spaniards raised a lusty cry: *"Por Santiago y por Dios!"* And they raced to their battle stations.

Aboard *HMS Prudence*, Lieutenant Wilberforce observed a disquieting sight through his telescope. "The Spaniard's running out his guns, sir."

Captain Biffing saw the gun ports yawn and the menacing barrels poke through. "Beat to quarters," he commanded.

"Beat to quarters!" called Lieutenant Wilberforce in a strangled scream.

The Marine drummer started the martial tattoo. The crew dashed to their battle stations, and the British gunners ran out their cannons. Captain Biffing struggled to estimate the distances between the two pitching and yawing ships. Math had never been his strong point. But artillery, he had always felt, was more a matter of dash than of math.

"Fire a shot across her bows, Lieutenant."

"Aye-aye, sir. Bow chaser!"

"Sir?" called the Forward Gunner.

"Aim over her bows," shrieked Lieutenant Wilberforce. "Higher. Higher." When he saw the gun was in position, he turned to Biffing and said, "Ready, sir."

"Fire at will," drawled Captain Biffing with studied insouciance.

"Fire!" screamed the Lieutenant.

The ball whistled over the slate-gray sea and splashed on the far side of the *Derechos de Hombre*.

"They're shooting at us," cried Ray.

Ilsa gripped his arm feverishly. "Isn't it exciting?"

Ray looked at her in disbelief. "No, it's not exciting. Are you out of your mind? Do you realize that if my crazy ancestor there gets shot and dies, I won't ever be born?"

"Well," said Ilsa haughtily, "I think it's exciting. Anyway, he's not going to die because here you are. Stop being such a grumpy baby."

Ray plunged into sobering thought. What would have happened if he had, by some cruel twist of fate, got hitched to this lunatic female? He could just see himself laying his head gently on his pillow, thinking, "O woman! When pain and anguish wring the brow, a ministering angel thou," when suddenly into the bedroom would leap this female Blackbeard, a parrot on her shoulder and a dagger in her teeth. He shuddered.

The *Derechos de Hombre* was running before the east wind on a westerly course. *HMS Prudence* was sailing northwest with the wind on her starboard beam. She was making better time than the Spaniard, but Don Raimondo had the vast ocean to maneuver in. He gave orders for his ship to aim for a place well ahead of Biffing's bow. Biffing was too late to see the danger, and when Don Raimondo reached his spot, he gave orders to wear around, so the wind filled his sails and sent him flying south along Biffing's port side. With the rain-streaked wind howling out of the east, both ships were heeling to the west. But this made the guns on the port side of *HMS Prudence* point uselessly down toward the waves, while it caused the guns of the *Derechos de Hombre* to tilt upward. And when the Spanish ship caught the English ship's lee, she straightened out, giving her a clean shot at the enemy's deck.

Don Raimondo ran down to the lower gun deck and supervised his crew manning the thirty-two-pounder cannons. "Fire as you bear!" he thundered. *"Fuego! Fuego! Fuego! Fuego!"* The *Derechos* raked *HMS Prudence* with a long broadside. Each gun discharged in a disciplined way, recoiling back into the lower gun deck and hissing with steam. Don Raimondo's shots wreaked hideous damage, bringing the sails and rigging of the foremast down with a crash and covering *HMS Prudence* in gray smoke.

Don Raimondo's ship continued on a southern tack, past the struggling British ship. He could probably have simply worn around and made a run for the coast. But who knows how crippled the other ship really was? With all that gold in his hold, he needed to finish her off and secure his escape. He scanned the field of battle and considered the wind. It was strong. The rigging was singing. So, Don Raimondo gave the order to change course from one tack to the other with the wind coming across his bow. It was a risky maneuver, because if he found himself in irons, he would be a sitting duck. But the speed of *Derechos de Hombre* was good. And so was that of the wind. The sails luffed for an anxious moment, but then they filled.

Don Raimondo made a full circle behind Biffing's stern and took a northern tack parallel to the starboard beam of the English ship. Biffing had failed to maneuver, and although he had not lost time in tacking as Don Raimondo had, with his foremast down and dragging, the Spaniard soon gained on him. *Derechos de Hombre* accelerated on a northbound course, with white water churning at her bow and foam rippling in her wake. Don Raimondo grinned. With reckless skill, the Count had put himself once again alongside the shattered port beam of *HMS Prudence*, while the starboard beam of *Derechos de Hombre*, bristling with still undischarged cannons, faced the enemy.

Biffing panicked. If he acted quickly, he thought, he might just cut across the Spaniard's bow. Or he might force the Spaniard to tack to the lee to avoid a collision.

"Helm a-lee! Helm a-lee, dammit!" shouted Captain Biffing.

"Helm a-lee!" repeated Wilberforce in a gurgling screech.

Timbers groaning, *HMS Prudence* began to wear around, but awkwardly, for her jibs had collapsed with the fallen foremast. But he had not acted quickly enough. Don Raimondo slid neatly alongside the Englishman, and, again, the wind caused both ships to heel to the west.

The two ships once more faced each other broadside, but with his ship heeling away from the wind, Don Raimondo's starboard guns again aimed upwards, the copper plating of his hull gleaming just above the waterline. Heeling with the wind, Biffing's port guns again pointed uselessly down toward the sea. Don Raimondo's starboard cannon were all primed and loaded. Biffing had not had time to clear the wreckage of his port side, drag away the wounded, and put his firepower back in order. As before, when the *Derechos de Hombre* slid into the British frigate's lee, it leveled off, its guns aiming straight into the tilted English deck. Biffing cringed. He felt what was coming.

"*Fuego! Fuego! Fuego!*" boomed the Count, running along his line of gunners on the lower gun deck, shouting encouragement, as the deafening broadside burst forth. Ilsa, with her hair flying and a crimson scarf tied around her neck, ran behind Don Raimondo, echoing him: "*Fuego! Fuego! Fuego!*" Ray goggled at her in disbelief. She looked like something out of a Goya painting of the Spanish Civil War. Of course, the Spanish Civil War hadn't happened yet. Perhaps Goya would use Ilsa as his model. The smoke belched from the cannon and obscured the deck of *HMS Prudence*. In a moment came the sickening whine and crack of timber, as Biffing's mainmast split and fell. The Spaniards cheered like pirates. *"Por Santiago!"*

Ilsa cheered. Ray was stunned. Chortling, Don Raimondo shot past his English foe. As he passed the gasping Englishman, he raised his hat gallantly to Captain Biffing and cried: "My compliments to King George!"

"Damn your eyes!" choked Biffing.

HMS Prudence was out of action. Don Raimondo gave the order to wear around and run before the wind to the Virginia shore. Biffing could only retaliate with his bow chaser.

"At least fire the bow chaser," yelled Biffing. "Fire!"

It went off musically, like a toy gun, hitting only the air behind the escaping Spaniard's stern.

As the prize ship bursting with Incan gold faded into the veils of mid-Atlantic rain, Lieutenant Wilberforce approached his Captain, who was surveying the shambles of his deck, tackle, and wounded crew. The Lieutenant tried to console his commander. "Look at the bright side, sir."

A homicidal, yellow gleam came into Biffing's eyes.

"We're still alive, sir," continued Wilberforce. "And you know, sir, if we've got our health, that's the main thing."

Captain Biffing goggled at the man, breathing asthmatically. "Our health?" he panted.

"Aye-aye, sir. Neither of us is shot."

It would have taken a man of sterner stuff than Captain Biffing to keep his pistol in his belt. Trembling with rage, he extracted it and aimed at his first officer. "I'll fix that!" he choked.

Edging away, the Lieutenant tried to soothe his Captain. "Sir, you're acting out of emotion. You'll feel better in the morning."

"I will if I do this!" shrieked Biffing. He squeezed the trigger. The hammer clicked softly. Nothing. Lieutenant Wilberforce laughed the relief of the reprieved. "You almost fooled me for a moment, sir! Ha! Ha! The powder's wet!"

"Aargh!" howled Biffing. He threw the pistol at Wilberforce, who ducked. The firearm pivoted picturesquely into the gray, choppy sea.

CHAPTER 12

OVER HILL, OVER DALE

Don Raimondo maneuvered his ship adroitly up the Potomac River and hove to just upstream from where the Anacostia River joins it. Ray and Ilsa gazed at the familiar, but unfamiliar, shore. "We're in Washington, D.C.," said Ilsa.

"Except there is no Washington, D.C. yet," said Ray gloomily.

"Think of it!" she said, reaching for Ray's hand. She had such a tiny hand. It felt nice, actually. But he was not over his bad mood. He withdrew his hand with a touch of frost.

The Spanish sailors ranged along the spars of the *Derechos*, and as the ship wheeled into the wind, the four-ton canvases of the foremast spluttered. The crew began furling the sails. The Count made a megaphone of his hands. "Down anchors!" The massive bower anchors slung from the catheads and plunged into the river with a splash that sent waves scrolling up the banks. Feliz looked at Don Raimondo and grinned. The Count smiled back at his faithful friend.

Don Raimondo lowered the pinnacle on davits over the side and into the river. Then he ordered a great treasure chest hauled out of the hold and onto the main deck. From there, he supervised the crew, lowering it into the pinnacle, which rocked rhythmically when the chest's weight settled into its planks. Ilsa gasped. The crest on the trunk was identical to the crest she had discovered on the ancient document in the National Archives. She pointed it out to Ray. He shrugged. Turning to the Count, she said, "Don Raimondo, that crest?"

"Our family crest, cousin," smiled the Count. That is my personal sea chest." With the eagerness of an overgrown boy, Don Raimondo leapt into the pinnacle. His impact made the craft rock like a cradle, and one of the sailors tumbled overboard. The crew on the deck above roared with laughter. "Hey, Ortiz," called one of the crew. "You cross the ocean but drown in a river!" The crew fished him out.

"This way, my dear," said the Count to Ilsa. And extending a gallant hand, he helped her aboard.

"Come on," called Ilsa to Ray, cheerily. He judged the distance between the ship and the pinnacle, took a deep breath, and leapt. He fell spread eagle across the thwarts. Trying to recover his dignity, he struggled up and brushed off his clothes. Ilsa and the Count laughed, quite unnecessarily, thought Ray.

"*Vamos, muchachos!*" cried Don Raimondo to his men. "Man the oars!" The pinnacle streaked across the shimmering Potomac as the sailors stroked with gusto.

"I've never seen the river so clean as this," said Ilsa. "It's as clear as gin."

"I wouldn't mind a shot of it," said Ray sullenly.

With a hush, the bow skidded up the sandy bank. Don Raimondo stepped ashore. He knelt and cupped the sand of the riverbank in his palm. He kissed it reverently. "The soil of freedom!" He turned to Ray, Ilsa, Feliz, and his men, holding the sand in his fist like a prize. "North America!"

The Spaniards cheered. Ilsa, carried away, cheered with them. The Count turned to her, took her by her slender waist, and hoisted her onto the beach without wetting her feet. Ray struggled over the pinnacle's gunwale and landed firmly in the Potomac mud. "Home at last," grumbled Ray, "but two hundred and forty-four years too soon."

"Oh, get over it," said Ilsa.

"Over it?" asked Ray coldly.

"Yes, over it," snapped Ilsa. "You'd think this was all my fault."

"Well, it is all your fault."

"Oh, it is, is it?"

"Of course it is. All I wanted to do was to take you out on a date."

"Well, you took me on a date."

"Yes, but for your dratted thesis. All you did was look at me like some kind of specimen, a butterfly pinned to a board."

"You consider yourself a butterfly?"

"I do."

"I should have thought something more like a beetle that crawled out from under a rock," said Ilsa, tossing her auburn hair.

"I suppose that's just the kind of specimen you would collect," said Ray acidly.

"Oh, that's what you think, is it?"

"Yes, it is."

"Well, you can think what you like," said Ilsa frigidly.

Ray wished he could think of a further retort that would sting, but nothing came to mind.

Don Raimondo led his team along the riverbank, exploring. Ray and Ilsa marched with them but on opposite sides of the trail. Pausing in the scrub, Feliz helped the Count don his morion helmet, cuirass, and steel shoulder plates. Ray also received a suit of armor. "Do I really have to wear this?" asked Ray.

"You do," said Don Raimondo. "For one thing, we are entering a field of battle."

"We are?" asked Ray unhappily.

"We are?" asked Ilsa breathlessly.

"Probably," said Feliz.

"But this weighs a ton," complained Ray.

"Bear up," said Don Raimondo. "You are an Almaviva, and even if this conquistador armor is a little out of date, it remains fashionable among the nobility. The American revolutionaries need to recognize our heritage and ronk."

"Wronk?" asked Ray.

"Yes, ronk," said Don Raimondo.

"What's wronk?" asked Ray.

"Station, prestige, position," said Don Raimondo, impatiently.

"Oh, rank," said Ray.

"That's what I said," said Don Raimondo.

"Well, can't we just tell them about it? She could tell them all about it," he said, jerking a thumb at Ilsa.

"No, no," said Don Raimondo. "People believe what people see. Our first impression must be inspiring."

"Well, of course, it must," said Ray sarcastically.

Ray donned the armor, and the Count of Almaviva gave the

signal for his small company to advance. Four men picked up a litter, bearing the treasure chest like the Ark of the Covenant. With stiff, military precision and muskets at the ready, the company marched along the riverbank.

Ray felt like a sardine in a tin. The cuirass, shoulder plates, and gauntlets clanked as he walked and made him sweat. Moreover, every now and then, little insects would find their way underneath this metal sheath and cause him to itch and tickle. He begged the Count to let him take it off and put it on again when circumstances required, but the Count forbade it. You never knew when they might be ambushed, he said.

"Oh, great," said Ray.

Soon, the Almavivan squad came to an Anacostank Indian village. Ilsa was thrilled to witness this civilization in its pristine state. After some wary bartering, the Indians offered their hospitality. Don Raimondo and Ray, with the help of Ilsa and Feliz, at last, doffed their armor. Then Don Raimondo, Ray, and Feliz enjoyed tobacco with the tribal leaders around a fire. Ilsa was not invited. After negotiating what he wanted from the chief, Don Raimondo sat back and relaxed.

"Excellent tobacco," he said.

"Yes," said the chief.

Don Raimondo placed a bag of gold *escudos* in the chief's hands. "This will do?"

The chief bit a gold coin. He was satisfied. "It will do."

"And who will take us to General Washington?"

Ilsa goggled. "*The* General Washington?" she asked.

"Is there another?" asked Don Raimondo.

The chief nodded to a tall, powerfully built brave.

"I know the way," said the brave.

"Good," said the Count. He mused for a moment. "Chief?"

"What?"

"I will send this brave back with double the gold if he does not betray us to the English. But," he added, pointing to the *Derechos de Hombre* silhouetted against the moon downriver, "my thirty-two pounders will be trained on this village until we safely return. If we do not safely return, there will be no more village."

The chief meditatively took his peace pipe from his thin, brown lips. "I don't know why you worry about the English," he drawled. "You are so very like them." Don Raimondo and the Indian Chief traded taut smiles.

The next day, after hours of weary tramping through Maryland in the miserably uncomfortable armor, Don Raimondo's company and the Indian guide paused to rest on a hilltop overlooking a charming valley. A few homesteads were scattered over the green landscape. The Indian guide was perfectly unfatigued, but Ray was panting under his metal attire.

"How far?" asked Ray.

"Very far," replied the brave.

Ray groaned.

"We must go *around* those farms," said Don Raimondo. "Through the woods. Our mission is secret."

The Indian guide assented.

"Do you recognize this line of the country?" Ilsa asked Ray.

"No," he replied. "No highways, no cities, no malls. I have no idea where we are."

"It's beautiful," she said, clasping her little hands in girlish delight.

"Oh, too beautiful," said Ray, summoning a bit more strength to carry on with his heavy armor.

Two days later, Don Raimondo's squad was trudging wearily up a country road when the Indian guide suddenly stiffened and halted.

"What is it?" asked Don Raimondo.

The Indian guide put his ear to the ground. The Spaniards watched him but milled about, making noisy footsteps.

"Hsh!" said the brave.

The Spaniards froze. The Indian listened awhile, then jumped up and made frantic gestures. "To the woods!"

"*Vamos! Ahora!*" ordered the Count.

The men hustled the treasure chest into the woods and crouched behind a spinney. Encased in armor, Ray found it difficult to crouch, but he did it. The clatter of hooves thundered up the road. A troop of British dragoons clattered by. Ray and Ilsa drank them in, Ray with anxiety, Ilsa with exuberance. Don Raimondo glanced at the Indian guide and nodded in approval. "Well done," he said.

The Indian guide smiled.

By the time they reached New Jersey, the Spaniards, carrying the heavy load of gold, were truly footsore. Ray was nearly dead, or at least he wished he were. But the team shuffled on.

"How far?" asked Ray, hoarsely.

"Not far now," smiled the Indian guide.

Ray pushed his conquistador helmet back over his hair and wiped his beaded brow. Ilsa smiled at him. He ignored her.

Suddenly the woods came alive with soldiers in tattered buckskins and hodgepodge uniforms. They leveled muskets at the Spaniards.

"Halt!" called an American soldier. "Hessians, Captain!" he cried.

Captain Frobish squinted at the bizarre, antiquated armor. "They ain't Germans," he mused, spitting. "And they ain't Lobsters. Who are ye?"

Don Raimondo stepped forward, formally. "Don Raimondo de Borbón y Cortés, Count of Almaviva and former Governor of His Most Catholic Majesty's colony, Santa Cecilia, at your service."

"What in tarnation?" cried a Virginian.

Captain Frobish scratched behind his ear. "Yer Spanish?"

"Castilian," said the Count. "Anyone can be Spanish. I wish you to present me to General Washington."

"You surrenderin'?" asked Captain Frobish.

"An Almavivan never surrenders. Do we, Ray?"

"I guess not," said Ray, without enthusiasm.

"I have an important gift for General Washington," continued the Count. He gestured toward the ornate trunk. Captain Frobish rubbed his grizzled chin.

"Hm..."

On the outskirts of Washington's camp near Monmouth, American pickets gawked at Captain Frobish's prisoners.

"Who goes there?" cried a sentinel.

"Bill, you damned fool, you can see it's me," said Frobish.

"But who're they?"

"Well, you've got eyes, ain't ya? They're my prisoners."

"How'd ya shoot 'em with all that armor?" asked Bill.

Captain Frobish drew himself up, indignant. "I didn't fire a shot. They knew better than to fiddle with a Massachusetts man!"

A crowd began to gather around the bizarrely armored Spaniards. Then a skinny, foppish young man got up from sipping coffee by a campfire and squinted incredulously at Don Raimondo.

"It can't be...," he said, with a markedly French accent. Then he blurted, "Don Raimondo?"

Don Raimondo turned at the sound of his name, scanning the men around him. Then he picked out the one who had called his name. "Lafayette!" shouted the Count.

"Cousin!" cried the Marquis.

"The Marquis de Lafayette," whispered Ilsa to Ray excitedly. He could have been the Grand Mufti of Jerusalem, for all Ray cared.

Embracing, the Europeans kissed each other's cheeks. The American soldiers recoiled in disgust.

"What are you doing here?" asked Lafayette.

"What are you doing here?" asked the Count.

"I am fighting with General Washington to secure the Rights of Man!" declared the Marquis.

"Me, too!" said Don Raimondo.

"Mais, non!"

"Pero, sí!"

"Does His Most Catholic Majesty, your cousin, know this?"

"I think he's probably heard of it by now," smiled the Spaniard.

"Ah! Then *mon cher....* " Lafayette broke into a song, singing tenor.

SONG: *THE RIGHTS OF MAN*

Lafayette: There's a whiff of revolution in the air.
You can't see it, you can't touch it, but it's there.
Every emperor and king
Shudders when he hears us sing
Of freedom's banner flying everywhere.

The Spaniards and the Americans joined in the chorus. Lafayette conducted them.

> All: So, hurrah for the rights of man!
> Equality is nature's plan.
> We're created to be free,
> And we'll never bend a knee,
> But fight for that great birthright,
> Our noble, global birthright,
> Our birthright since the world began.

Don Raimondo added his sonorous baritone to Lafayette's tenor for the second verse.

> All: Oh, there is something going 'round that you can feel.
> An upheaval too colossal to conceal.
> Soon the old will pass away
> With the dawning of a day
> When every dream of justice will be real.

Captain Frobish muscled in and joined the two noblemen for the third verse.

> All: Oh, we will never let a government repress
> Our opportunities for welfare and success.
> We won't mindlessly obey
> Or let them tax our wealth away
> For their palaces and wars and fancy dress.

Utterly swept away by the *esprit de corps,* the entire camp joined in a final chorus.

> All: So, hurrah for the rights of man!
> Equality is nature's plan.

We're created to be free,

And we'll never bend a knee,

But fight for that great birthright,

Our noble, global birthright,

Our birthright since the world began.

Everyone let out a cheer that made the trees rattle. Don Raimondo mopped his brow with a handkerchief, and asked Lafayette, "Will you present me to His Excellency, the great Washington?"

"Bien sûr!"

Lafayette clasped Don Raimondo's hand and grinned.

CHAPTER 13

GENERAL WASHINGTON'S WAR

In green fields not far away, General George Washington was losing the War of Independence. Puffs of smoke drifted over a meadow where he sat his horse with conspicuous grace. He scanned his ranks. The colonial soldiers stood frozen, waiting for the artillery smoke to clear and wondering if, in the recent cannonade, they had been hit; they were amateurs in the art of war. This might be their moment to fall down with blood-curdling shrieks. Or possibly not. They stared at each other, fogged, waiting for a cue. None of them did fall down, as it happened, for the Hessians were miserable shots, even on the rare occasions when they were sober (of which this fearful battle assuredly was not one).

In his gentle, Virginia accents, Washington called the men to charge the enemy line. Then a second enemy volley boomed across the field. What the Hessians lacked in accuracy, they made up for in volume. After all, the English Parliament was paying for the shot, and the German King of England would expect them to get his money's worth. Besides, the simple creatures enjoyed the thunder of guns.

Smoke obscured the lines again. When it cleared, Washington found himself alone on the field. Yankee practical thinking had prevailed. Washington's army had scampered into the woods. In acute embarrassment, Washington stole a glance at his more professional English counterpart on the opposite heights. Then he spied a sly Scottish marksman drawing a bead on his blue wool coat. The Father of His Country stiffened in the saddle. If he were to die today, it would be in defiance. The English officer tapped the Scottish sharpshooter's musket with his drawn sword. Sniping officers, even colonial officers, simply wasn't done. The Scottish marksman lowered his barrel in disgust.

Washington's muscles relaxed. The trace of a smile wandered over his thin lips. He touched the corner of his hat with two fingers. The English officer deigned to return the salute, indulging, however, in a supercilious sneer. With as much aplomb as he could muster, the American General pivoted his horse and followed his prudent soldiery into the great, primeval woods.

As he rode, Washington reflected bitterly. He was short of money, gunpowder, shot, and food. All he had going for him was The Cause, the Rights of Man. Very noble and all that. But just add a whiff of money, gunpowder, shot, and food, and the old Cause might really click. Congress had pledged more help, of course, which, knowing Congress, meant that the aid might come in a decade or so after the war was lost. He sighed and gazed heavenward.

Was a tiny miracle too much to ask?

Back inside his tent, George Washington pored over a tattered map of New Jersey and New York, rubbing his temples. His aide brought him a cup of tea.

"Tea will ease your headache, sir."

"I'm afraid tea is much the cause of it," sighed Washington.

Captain Frobish presented himself at the door of the tent, coughing discreetly. "Visitors, General."

"Not now, please."

The Marquis de Lafayette burst in flamboyantly. *"Mon générale!* I am too delighted to present to you my noble cousin, the Count of Almaviva."

Wearily, Washington rose and donned his coat. Ray and Ilsa, who also trickled in, were struck by how impressively tall he was.

"I am honored, sir," said Washington wearily.

Bowing stiffly, the Count announced himself. "Don Raimondo de Borbón y Cortés, Count of Almaviva and former Governor of His Most Catholic Majesty's colony, Santa Cecilia, and the honor, Your Excellency, is all mine."

To Washington's acute discomfort, Don Raimondo planted a kiss on both of his weather-beaten cheeks.

"And these are my cousins," said Don Raimondo, "Ray and Ilsa Almaviva."

They weren't cousins at all, thought Ray, and Ilsa, as a matter of fact, wasn't even related. It pained him to reflect that they were foisting this imposture on a man who could not tell a lie.

"How can I help you?" replied Washington, warily.

"I believe, *mon cher générale,*" said Lafayette, "that my illustrious cousin is here to help you."

Washington arched a skeptical brow. So far, he was undecided about which was worse: warring with Europeans or working with them. But life's complexities never dulled the edge of his fine, Virginia manners. "May I entreat you to share my supper, sirs and madam?"

The Spaniard and the Frenchman bowed as if they had been invited to the Escorial or Versailles. Ray sat unceremoniously at the table, but all the other gentlemen remained standing until the well-bred General pulled out a chair for the only lady present and seated Ilsa. Embarrassed, Ray stood up and then resumed his seat only when the others had taken theirs.

After dinner, during which the garrulous Don Raimondo and Lafayette had dominated the conversation with gossip from the chanceries of Europe, their host apologized for the humble fare.

"The fortunes of war," said Lafayette philosophically.

"General Washington," said Don Raimondo, "may I come to the point?"

"Ah, my dear cousin," said Lafayette, "you will find that General Washington always likes coming to the point. A man of action! And few words."

"I am all ears, my dear Count," said Washington.

Don Raimondo folded his napkin nicely. "King Carlos appointed me governor of the strategic island of Santa Cecilia in the Caribbean."

"I know it," said Washington.

"Ah, yes. Your Excellency once lived in Martinique."

Washington nodded.

"Well, I heard of your brave struggle for liberty against the English King, and I thought, somehow, I must lend a hand." Don Raimondo told the tale of how he had hijacked the Peruvian gold. Washington and Lafayette listened, speechless and entranced. "And so," concluded the Count, "I marched hundreds of miles north from the Potomac River with the help of my dear cousins and my loyal crew, and here I am."

"*Extraordinaire!*" cried Lafayette.

The Count then opened his treasure chest dramatically. Washington and Lafayette involuntarily shot from their chairs at the sight of the great, glimmering trove of Spanish gold.

"*Mon Dieu!*" said the Marquis.

"Good Lord!" said Washington.

"For you," said Don Raimondo.

Washington stared at the man. "For me, sir?"

"For the Cause, Your Excellency! For the Rights of Man! And there is much, much more in the hold of my ship."

Lafayette clapped Don Raimondo on the back and grinned ecstatically at Washington. But the General's brow was creased with concern.

CHAPTER 14

THE PROPOSAL

The next morning, Washington and Don Raimondo took a ride through the woods, alone. Washington, a splendid horseman, sailed over stone walls and fallen logs, as if his horse, like Pegasus, had wings. After a bit of stimulating exercise, the riders broke into a gentle trot and talked.

"We certainly need the gold," said Washington. "If only the British knew it, we are flat out of gunpowder, and we don't have enough saltpeter in the colonies to make it. And we have no bullets nor the metal to cast them. The French and the Dutch won't take our money. Continental money might be worth nothing if we lose. So gold is our only hope."

"And now you have it," smiled Don Raimondo.

"But what do you want?"

Don Raimondo affected a wounded look. "To fight by your side. To see the cause of human rights, prevail over the tyranny of kings."

"Yes, yes, of course," said Washington. "But what do you personally want?"

Don Raimondo smiled. "Well, since you mention it, one little thing."

Washington reined his horse to a stop. Don Raimondo also drew rein. They sat for a moment, studying each other's features, the one stony with tired eyes, the other swarthy, with eyes dancing.

"Your Excellency, I am a count. Of royal blood. But I have committed piracy and treason for the sake of your cause."

"No one asked you to."

"True. I did it gladly. But I can never go back."

Washington pursed his thin lips grimly. "None of us can. As Dr. Franklin has said, if we do not hang together, we shall all hang separately."

"Yes. So I ask only one little thing."

"Yes?"

"Your land on the Potomac River is beautiful."

"It is."

"I ask only for a little piece of it. A few square miles to call my own, and settlements for my men, there, on the Potomac, where I first touched shore."

"A landholding?" asked Washington, relieved. "I think, in return for your extraordinary donation to The Cause, that should not be a problem."

"But one other thing...a tiny thing."

George Washington sighed. "Why is always one other tiny thing in this impossible war?" he complained.

"But this is so easy for you, my dear General. You see, I am a count and a nephew of the King. It would hardly do for me to have no ronk."

"Wronk?" asked Washington.

"Yes, ronk," said Don Raimondo.

"What's wronk?" asked Washington.

"Nothing's wrong," said Don Raimondo.

"No, I mean, what did you mean by having no ronk?" asked Washington.

Don Raimondo heaved a deep sigh. "Station. Prestige. Position," he said.

"Oh, rank," said Washington.

"That's what I said," said Don Raimondo, murmuring to himself, "Does no one speak proper English up here?"

"I can make you a colonel," said Washington.

"I'm afraid that would be a step down."

"I suppose I could make you a general, but there would be the deuce to pay with my other officers."

"What I had in mind," said Don Raimondo, "was a duke."

Washington goggled at the man. "A duke?"

"Yes," smiled the Spaniard. "That's one up from a count."

Washington slashed the air with his hand. His patience finally had run out. "But we're fighting against the divine right of kings! Do you appreciate the irony of our fighting a war against the titled nobility of Europe while making you an American duke?"

"Yes," replied Don Raimondo, fastidiously studying his nails. "It is almost as ironic as fighting a war without gunpowder or bullets."

His eyes met Washington's eyes. The two men studied each other for a moment of troubled silence.

"Don Raimondo…"

"General Washington…"

Washington massaged his temples. The headache was back.

"I shall refer the matter to the Congress in Philadelphia. They are honorable men. They will find a way to do what is needed without compromising our principles."

"Of course, Your Excellency," said Don Raimondo. "I would wish it no other way."

CHAPTER 15

THE TITLE DEED

Old Philadelphia was charming, and the society, Don Raimondo noted approvingly, was urbane. Ray was glad to be free of his conquistador armor, as he wandered through the Continental Capital. Ilsa was like a kid in a candy store. "Do you realize we're seeing it, really seeing it, American history as it was?"

"I keep hoping we're dreaming," said Ray.

"Look," cried Ilsa, pointing at a building. "I believe, I think, if I'm not wrong, that's the home of Benjamin Franklin."

"Super," said Ray.

"Shall we knock on his door?" asked Ilsa.

"Suppose he gave at the office?" asked Ray. But Ilsa had already bounded over to the front steps. A servant woman answered the door and looked them over warily. "And who might you two be?"

"This is Ray Almaviva, cousin of the famous Count Almaviva," said Ilsa, "the man who brought America the Spanish gold."

"Ma'am," said Ray, nodding respectfully.

"And I'm the Queen of Sheba," said the servant. "Wait here. I shall enquire if King Solomon will see you." And off she went. After a few moments, Ben Franklin appeared at the door and scanned his unexpected guests up and down. "You are the cousins of that Spanish grandee General Washington sent us?"

"We are, sir," said Ilsa.

"Well, then, enter. A true friend is the best possession."

"Ah, *Poor Richard's Almanack*, 1744," said Ilsa, quoting Franklin's published writing as excitedly as a contestant on a game show.

Franklin smiled. "Very good, m'dear."

"I have read every edition," said Ilsa.

"And you, sir?" enquired Franklin of Ray.

"I, sir, am a political scientist."

"Good to meet a fellow soul!" laughed Franklin, pumping Ray's hand. Franklin led them into his drawing room and called for the female servant. "Would you kindly bring our guests some coffee?" he asked. She looked none too pleased, but she complied. "She's a bit of a crank," said Franklin, "but I keep her because no one else can bear with my eccentricities."

"Oh, I'm sure you're exaggerating," protested Ilsa.

"He that would live in peace and at ease must not speak all he knows or judge all he sees," said Franklin.

"*The Almanack*, 1734," said Ilsa.

"Very good," laughed Franklin. "And you," he asked Ray, "are you sure you have not read *Poor Richard's Almanack?*"

"I'm afraid not," said Ray. "But," he added, "I have always been fascinated by your kite experiment with electricity."

"In 1752," said Ilsa, excitedly.

"In, as you correctly say, 1752," said Franklin. "What would you like to know about it, m'boy?"

"Well," said Ray, "you didn't discover electricity, exactly, did you?"

"No, certainly not," said Franklin. "Scientists have known about electricity for thousands of years. The point was to demonstrate that lightning *is* electrical energy."

"So you flew a kite," said Ray.

"Made of a silken handkerchief," said Franklin. "With a length of wire on top. And a hemp string, moistened by the rain, tied to a dry silk string, which I held standing inside a barn, out of the rain, so it would remain dry."

"So, the moistened hemp rope conducted electricity?" asked Ray.

"Right. But the dry silk string didn't. And to the hempen rope, I attached a large metal key."

"And then you flew the kite up into the storm," said Ray.

"With my son, William," said Franklin. "And we waited and waited. I was near to despairing that anything would happen, even though there was a great tempest. Then I saw the hairs of the hempen rope standing up on end like quills on a hedgehog. I was thrilled. I held my hand out toward the key, and as the negative charges in the metal were attracted to the positive charges in my hand, I felt the spark." Franklin slapped his knee and let out a guffaw. The servant, who was bringing in the coffee, nearly dropped her tray. "Using a Leyden jar, I collected the electric fire very copiously for later use," he said, terribly pleased with himself.

"What's a Leyden jar?" asked Ilsa.

"It's a primitive kind of battery," said Ray.

"Not so primitive as all that, m'boy," said Franklin.

"So the lightning never actually struck your kite?" asked Ray.

"Oh no," chuckled Franklin. "Had it done so, I probably would not be here to tell you the tale."

"I don't know how long we are staying," said Ray, "but I would love to help you conduct that experiment again."

"Certainly, if you like," said Franklin, "although," he added, pouring out coffee for his newfound friends, "I am afraid the storms in Philadelphia these days are more political than climatic. Right up your alley, m'boy," he said to Ray.

"No gains without pains," quoted Ilsa.

"*The Almanack*, 1745," said Benjamin Franklin. He and Ilsa shared a laugh.

The next day, Don Raimondo, Ray, and Ilsa went to Independence Hall. They were accompanied by Feliz and three of the crew from the *Infanta*, who carried the Count's heavy chest of gold and deposited it within the meeting chamber. There they met Franklin, John Adams, James Madison, John Hancock, Thomas Jefferson, and Samuel Chase. The Founders stood beside a cherry wood table on which a large document lay open. At the bottom of the ornate scroll gleamed the signatures of all six Founders.

"Can you believe we're actually seeing this?" Ilsa whispered to Ray. He didn't like to admit it, but it was rather exciting.

"We are honored," said John Adams, "that Mr. Jefferson has consented to travel to Philadelphia from Monticello to assist at this signing ceremony."

"Ah, Mr. Jefferson, the author of those inspiring words," said Don Raimondo, "'we hold these truths to be self-evident, that all men are created equal, that they are endowed by their Creator with certain inalienable rights, that among these are life, liberty, and the pursuit of happiness.'"

"Unalienable," corrected Jefferson softly.

"Inalienable," corrected Adams, petulantly.

"John, I shall not stay to argue this again," said Jefferson.

"All right, Thomas," said Adams, "all right."

"To business," said Jefferson.

"Mr. Chase," said Franklin, "has generously won the approval of his colony to cede forty-four thousand acres on the north bank of the Potomac River in the name of The Cause."

"Maryland," said Chase grandly, "constitutes millions of acres. A few hundred will not be missed."

"You are too kind," said Don Raimondo. "And this parcel shall be entitled?"

"The Duchy of Almaviva," said John Hancock, with a flourish.

"With rights and title," said Madison, "to be conferred upon your heirs in perpetuity, as you requested."

Ilsa and Ray exchanged awestruck glances.

"But we all understand," warned Jefferson, "that this in no way represents a compromise of our Republican principles."

"Absolutely not!" cried Don Raimondo.

"Heaven forbid!" said Hancock.

"Perish the thought!" said Chase.

"And it is not a question of the money," said Jefferson.

"By no means!" cried Madison.

"I would challenge any man to a duel who suggested it!" thundered Don Raimondo.

"Now, everyone must pledge," said Franklin, "that this Act of our Committee shall remain a secret in time of war. The enemy must not know we have obtained these funds. We will make a public proclamation when victory is ours. Agreed?"

Everyone murmured their assent.

James Madison neatly scrolled up the parchment and handed it to the Spaniard. "Then here is your title and deed, Your Grace."

"I thank Your Excellencies. And there," said the American Duke, opening his treasure chest, "is but one of the many chests of America's gold."

The glistening ore burned red in the morning sun. Its glow shimmered on the walls of Independence Hall. There, in that chest, the Founders saw gunpowder, muskets, balls, victuals, shoes, and, above all, hope. They declared, in chorus, "Long live the American Duke!"

CHAPTER 16

THE AWFUL TRUTH

As presumed siblings, Ray and Ilsa had been given a single room. It was a little awkward. Ray couldn't help sometimes feeling a shiver of desire for Ilsa in such close quarters, but his injured pride quickly snuffed out the aspiring flame. Ilsa was impressed that Ray, who had been so seductive when they first met, was behaving like a perfect gentleman, more perfect, Ilsa sometimes felt, than she would have liked. What was in the air that night, however, was not romance, but an exhilaration which, in her mind, transcended their checkered relationship.

"You see the point?" gasped Ilsa, her breath coming short. "You are the ancestor of the American Duke. No, you actually *are* a duke!"

"How can that really be?" asked Ray.

"We saw it with our own eyes," said Ilsa. "They gave your ancestor a title deed. And forty-four thousand acres on the north side of the Potomac. That's more than sixty-eight square miles. Do you know what that means?"

"I'm in real estate?" asked Ray.

"No! You rightfully own Washington, D.C.," said Ilsa. "All of it."

They sat for a moment in stunned silence.

"But how is that possible?" asked Ray. "What happened to the title deed? The land in D.C. has been bought and sold a million times. They couldn't just ignore the title deed."

"Don't you see?" said Ilsa. "They forgot about it. Or they hushed it up. Did you hear what Franklin said in Independence Hall? The whole thing must be kept secret—a military secret in time of war. And remember what I told you about Don Raimondo? He died in Austria, fighting with Napoleon at the Battle of Austerlitz."

"When was that?" asked Ray.

"It hasn't happened yet, obviously, because he's still here. It will be in 1805. It was Napoleon's greatest victory."

"But what has Don Raimondo got to do with Napoleon?" asked Ray.

"You see what a fanatic he is about the rights of man and all that," said Ilsa.

"Well, we all care about our rights," said Ray.

"Yes, but did you ever think of robbing the Treasury for the rights of man?"

"No, because unlike you and him, I'm not out of my mind."

"And who gets away with something like that?" persisted Ilsa. "He did. What an ancestor you had," she rhapsodized. Eying Ray critically, she added, "You should be more like him."

"Oh, I should, should I? Well, let me tell you something..."

"He's a relative of Lafayette," interrupted Ilsa. "And they're chums. After the American Revolution, Lafayette went back and championed the French Revolution. He probably convinced Don Raimondo to go with him. When Napoleon became emperor, he lost Lafayette's support, but Don Raimondo must have remained a fan, because he gave his life at Austerlitz for the French Empire."

"You're just guessing at all this," said Ray.

"Maybe some of it," said Ilsa, "but it makes sense, and, anyway, all that really matters is that he became the first and only American Duke, got the title deed to the District of Columbia, and died in Europe. He must have had children, of course, because here you are, but he must have had them in France, and their descendants must have come back to the United States later, without knowing about the title of duke. Then your grandfather's orphanage burned down, and the trail went cold."

"Until you picked up the scent," said Ray.

"Yep," said Ilsa, triumphantly.

"I guess you'll get your tenure with this story," said Ray. "If we ever get back."

"Well," said Ilsa. "If we do, here's the most important thing we have to do: go back to the National Archives and get our hands on that title deed."

Ray went to the window and looked out into the quiet, dark Philadelphia street.

"You think we ever will get back?" asked Ray.

"I really don't see how," said Ilsa. "But we'd better, or you'll never be born."

"Neither will you."

"I guess not."

CHAPTER 17

EXPERIMENTING WITH DR. FRANKLIN

Don Raimondo was sitting for a portrait by the famous Revolutionary painter, John Trumbull. He was dressed in his antique conquistador armor for the painting, commemorating his proud descent from Cortés, the conqueror of Mexico. The humid summer air in Philadelphia made the long sessions exceedingly uncomfortable, and when he could stand it no longer, Don Raimondo raised a gauntleted hand. "Thank you, *Señor* Trumbull. May we continue tomorrow?"

Trumbull was a little put out. He was an artist and, therefore, naturally petulant. But Don Raimondo was a singularly important and very wealthy person, who had paid for the portrait in advance, so he acquiesced. The Duke stretched his limbs.

"Shall I help Your Grace out of your armor?" asked Trumbull.

"Thank you. That will not be necessary. I have a coach waiting. I will disrobe in my lodgings."

"Very good, Your Grace."

The Duke marched a little stiffly out the front door. People stared to see this re-incarnation of Pizarro in a Philadelphia street, but Don Raimondo was too wrapped in hidalgo pride to pay them any notice. His coach and four were waiting at the door, and with some creaking difficulty, he climbed inside. The coach sagged under the heavy armor. Don Raimondo bore up in the sweaty encasement. The humidity of this wretched city did not make it easy. But he was refreshed as storm clouds began to gather and a brisk wind swept in from the northeast.

Dr. Franklin arrived at the lodgings of Ray and Ilsa, bearing a giant, silken kite and wearing an impish grin. "The weather," he told them jovially, "is inclement but at the same time opportune. Shall we reproduce my experiment?"

"That would be wonderful!" cried Ray. Ilsa agreed. The clip-clop of sixteen hooves rang on the cobblestones as Don Raimondo's ducal carriage rolled up to the lodgings. The Duke descended, his ceremonial armor clanking.

"Your Grace," said Franklin, "Why don't you join us? We are about to reproduce my kite flying experiment, of which Your Grace may possibly have heard."

Don Raimondo grinned from ear to ear. "Who has not heard of that? But may I first get out of this armor?"

"I'm afraid," said Franklin, glancing at the gathering black clouds which were shimmering with lightning, "that the moment is at hand."

"Lost time is never found again," quoted Ilsa.

"*The Almanack*, 1747," said Franklin, grinning.

"Come along, Your Grace," said Ray, "you mustn't miss it."

"Very well, cousin," conceded the Duke. Franklin led the group to a barn around the back of the lodgings. Thunder began to murmur. Franklin handed the kite to Ray. "Will you do the honor, sir?"

Ray nodded, trembling with excitement. He took the kite and ran a few yards away. Then he hurled it into the air. The wind caught it, and it wobbled upward as Franklin paid out lengths of the hempen rope. Finally, it attained a fine height and, pulling at its cord, flew stoutly in the brisk northeasterly wind.

"Come in here," said Franklin to Ray, gesturing toward the shelter. Ray ran over to the barn, and he, Ilsa, Don Raimondo, and Dr. Franklin all huddled inside as raindrops the size of pennies began to hail down from heaven.

"And now we wait," said Franklin.

"May I hold the cord?" asked Ray, forgetting his former gloom.

"You may indeed," said Franklin.

Ray took the cord and felt the tugging of the recalcitrant kite. Looking through the crack in the barn door, he saw it valiantly straddling the breeze. Lightning flashed to the left and right. With exhilaration, Ray noticed the fibers on the hempen rope tingle and stand on end.

"It's happening!" he cried.

"What's happening?" asked Don Raimondo.

"The electricity from the ambient lightning is empowering the wet hempen rope," said Ray.

"Exactly," grinned Franklin.

"Now," said Ray, "if we just touch the key attached to it, we shall feel the spark."

Ray, Ilsa, and Don Raimondo huddled closely together, watching the prickling hempen cord with fascination. Dr. Franklin, amused, stepped back to clean his eyeglasses with a large silk handkerchief. Don Raimondo extended his right hand, still encased in the armorial gauntlet, to touch the key. Franklin started in alarm. "No! No!" he cried.

But it was too late. The Duke touched the key. Lightning struck the kite and sizzled down the hempen cord. Don Raimondo's armored forearm lit up like St. Elmo's fire, covering the walls of the barn with sheets of light and momentarily blinding Franklin. In a crackling blast, and then a sizzle and pop, Ray, Ilsa, and Don Raimondo disappeared. Smoke filled the barn, and the kite went sailing off into the angry skies. Blinking, Dr. Franklin gazed in horror at the grease spot that marked the last stand of his three vanished friends.

Part Three

Democracy substitutes election
by the incompetent many for
appointment by the corrupt few.

—George Bernard Shaw

CHAPTER 18

ARRESTED FOR CONSPIRACY

Ray, Ilsa, and Don Raimondo staggered to their feet. Ray and Ilsa, glancing around, recognized Washington, D.C.. They were back. Don Raimondo was agog. "What happened?" he asked. "Where are we?"

It took a moment for Ray and Ilsa to find speech. At last, Ray said, "We are back in our time and place."

"I don't understand," said Don Raimondo.

"Let's go to my house," said Ray. "And have a drink."

"Your Grace, take off the armor, please," said Ilsa. "People around here won't understand."

"Where is around here? What people?" asked the Duke, shuddering.

"Trust me, cousin," said Ray.

He did trust them. They unclasped his armor, and each took a piece of it. He tucked the curved helmet under his arm.

"Come along," said Ilsa, smiling bravely to comfort him, even though she felt quite shaken. Ray, in spite of everything, had to admire her courage and caring touch. The Duke nodded and followed them, with a demeanor rather more like a plucked rooster than his formerly swashbuckling self. But when they came to a street, and automobiles whizzed past, Don Raimondo leapt in the air like a startled cat. "What are those?" he cried.

"Cars," said Ilsa. "We don't use horses anymore."

Don Raimondo stared in disbelief. When they reached Ray's apartment, Ray switched on the electric lights. Again, Don Raimondo leapt in shock. "How did you do that?" he asked.

"That little experiment we conducted with Dr. Franklin," said Ray, "it allowed us to harness electricity and turn it into electric light."

"Wonderful," said Don Raimondo, smiling for the first time since his transmigration. He curiously flicked the light switch on and off, several times. "Wonderful," he murmured.

"OK, stop that," said Ray irritably.

They set his precious armor on a chair and sat down.

"Shall I make coffee?" said Ilsa.

"I think whisky would be better," said Ray.

"So do I," agreed the Duke.

Ray brought a restorative flask and three glasses. The trio drank a stiff one gratefully.

"Now, please tell me what I need to know," said Don Raimondo, steeling himself for the worst.

"Well," said Ray, "it isn't 1776 anymore."

Don Raimondo stared at him. From what he had seen so far, that did seem to be the case.

"It's two hundred and forty-four years in the future: the year 2021."

The Duke held out his glass for another shot. Ray sympathetically poured him a double. Then the Duke erupted in hearty laughter. "So that's the date. What is the place?"

"This is the District of Columbia, the capital city of the United States of America," said Ilsa.

"The United..." the Duke's voice trailed away. "So Washington did win his war!"

"With your help," said Ilsa.

"And the country has lasted this long?" asked Don Raimondo.

"Not only that," said Ilsa, "it has become the richest and most powerful country on earth."

The Duke emitted a low whistle. Then a thought struck him. "But where is my Duchy?"

Ray and Ilsa exchanged glances.

"Right here," said Ray. "We're in it."

Don Raimondo was puzzled. "I thought you said this was some place called the District of Columbia."

"It is," said Ray. "Right on top of where your Duchy used to be."

"Used to be!" barked Don Raimondo, standing in indignation. "Is! Congress granted it to me in perpetuity!"

"Let me explain," said Ilsa. But before she could do so, there was a tremendous crack, and the door to Ray's place flew open. Agent Schweppes and a dozen FBI agents in body armor and bearing high-powered weapons crashed into the apartment.

"On your knees!" shouted Schweppes.

Ray and Ilsa were too stunned to move.

"On your knees!" he shouted again as the agents pushed them

down. They tried to floor Don Raimondo, but he resisted. "This is an outrage!" he cried.

Four agents ganged up on Ray, handcuffed him, and led him away.

"Where are you taking him?" cried Ilsa.

The agents made no reply.

"*Why* are you taking him?" she asked.

Special Agent in Charge Schweppes turned before following his men down the stairs of the front stoop.

"Trying to foment insurrection," he said, with a sadistic grin. "We don't tolerate that." Then he turned on his heel and was gone.

CHAPTER 19

PROOF

Even though Ilsa had explained everything to Don Raimondo several times, actually, he remained in a state of stunned disbelief. But he agreed with her absolutely that the next vital step was to find his missing title deed. It was the only way to free Ray. To that end, he and Ilsa made their way through the streets of the capital to the National Archives.

Everything was astonishing to the poor Duke. They passed a pair of girls with pink and purple hair, nose piercings, and shredded jeans. He clucked his tongue.

"Are they witches?" he asked Ilsa. "Or insane?"

Ilsa smiled. "No, it's just their style."

"Style?" said the Duke. "No, my dear, the lack of it."

As they waited at a crosswalk, a car pulled up to them with hip-hop music blaring.

"Good God," cried the Duke. "What is that noise?"

"It's a kind of music," said Ilsa.

"It is no kind of music," said Don Raimondo. "I have heard better music from natives up the Orinoco."

Ilsa realized that acclimatizing the Duke to the twenty-first century was going to be much harder than it took her and Ray to acclimatize to the eighteenth. Looking backwards, however traumatic as at times it may be, is nowhere near as unsettling as seeing the future. This, Ilsa supposed, is why God created time—so everything wouldn't happen all at once.

When she presented her credentials and gained access once again to the room full of historical documents, the two began searching the chamber. They now had the advantage of knowing exactly what document they were seeking, and they soon found it, scrolled up, covered in dust, ignored, and forgotten for over two centuries. Don Raimondo ran his fingers over it lovingly. "My Duchy of Almaviva," he said dreamily. Then to Ilsa, he said, "What do we do now?"

"Well," she said, "I hate to risk creasing such an ancient document, but it can't be helped. We have to smuggle it out of here. We have to have it validated, and then I will publish an article on the internet. Publish or perish, you see. Now more than ever. Would you mind turning around?"

"Turning around?"

"I have to conceal the document under my blouse. If I put it in my purse, they might search that."

"Of course," said the Duke. A paragon of chivalry, he turned away as Ilsa opened her blouse, wrapped the frail deed gingerly around her waist, and buttoned her blouse again. "All set," she said, and the two made their way toward the exit, Ilsa crackling softly.

As it happened, an employee did search Ilsa's purse. She and Don Raimondo exchanged knowing glances. They made it, however, into the open air, and Ilsa hailed a cab. Don Raimondo was much alarmed at riding in the taxi, but he soon became fascinated with the electric windows and began buzzing them up and down, up and down.

"Would you cut it out, bud?" asked the taxi driver.

"Cut what out?" asked the Duke. "What does he want me to cut?" he asked Ilsa.

"He means stop playing with the window."

"Oh, sorry," said Don Raimondo.

The cab left them off at the university. Ilsa led Don Raimondo hurriedly inside one of the buildings and down the corridor to a lab. There she met a friend, a forensic historian, Sunil Deshmukh, a friend she could trust.

"Hello, Ilsa," said Sunil cordially.

"Hi," she said, out of breath. "Listen, Sunil, I need your help and fast. Oh, this is my friend, um, my cousin, Raimondo, by the way."

"Nice to meet you," said Sunil, adjusting the glasses on the bridge of his nose.

"Listen, Sunil, would you turn around?" asked Ilsa.

"What?"

"Let's both turn around," said Don Raimondo.

As they did so, Ilsa slipped the ancient title deed from under her blouse and laid it on one of Sunil's lab tables.

"Oh, an old document. Marvelous," beamed Sunil.

"I want you to validate its authenticity," said Ilsa. "You know, type of paper and ink, handwriting, all that sort of thing. I want you to verify that it is a real, eighteenth-century document. Can you do that?"

"Well, of course," said Sunil. He consulted his calendar. "How about you come back for it in a week?"

"Can you do it today?"

"Today!" exclaimed Sunil. "Ilsa, these things take time."

"There is no time, Sunil. You must do it right away."

"What's the rush?" he asked.

"It's the biggest story in the world right now, but only if you can validate the document."

"Ah," he smiled. "Well, you interest me strangely. Let's get to it, then. We're going to look at the paper, the ink, the handwriting, and the grammar. That should do it if anything can."

"You're a real pal," said Ilsa, patting his arm.

With Ilsa and Don Raimondo leaning over his shoulders, Sunil began his examination. "The paper looks authentic," he said. Carefully taking a fine pair of tweezers, he extracted a bit of the paper's fiber and placed it under a microscope. Ilsa and the Duke followed him over to the instrument. "Hmm," Sunil grunted. "Ah."

"Well?" asked the Duke.

"The paper is discolored, but from the pattern of discoloration and the various hues, I would be prepared to say the discoloration is, in fact, from age, not chemical dye or other artificial contaminants."

"So it is from the eighteenth century?" asked Ilsa.

"Of course it is," said the Duke. "We saw them…"

Ilsa laid a finger severely beside her nose. Don Raimondo swallowed the rest of his sentence.

"Well, I can't say exactly what year the paper was rolled, but I can say that it is old. Perhaps two hundred years old, and possibly more. Not more recent than that."

"Excellent," said Ilsa. "And the ink?"

"Ink is a very complicated subject, especially when you are writing with a quill pen. In order not to coagulate and keep the quill pen flowing, it should be iron gall ink. It should be made of oak apples, which are pure tannic acid, with green vitriol or iron sulfate, which, when mixed together, produce a blue-black fluid, bound together with gum Arabic. So, let's see."

Sunil searched the document with a high-powered magnifying glass. He located a bit of writing with a broad loop in the calligraphy and, taking a scalpel, he chipped off a bit of the ink as a sample. "Sorry," he said to Ilsa.

"Go ahead; it's worth it," she replied.

Sunil placed the ink spot on a bit of paper in a planar thin-layer chromatograph. He then released the solvents and watched the ink extend into various color bands. He smiled with satisfaction. "Of course, with such a small sample, you don't get long bands, but we have enough here to show that the fingerprint of this ink fits an eighteenth-century profile. You're two for two, Ilsa," Sunil said. "As for the handwriting, that's rather simple. Obviously, a counterfeiter could imitate the careful calligraphy of the 1700s, but what we can say is that this handwriting conforms to the period. The grammar is also consistent. Again, an imposter could counterfeit that, but combining the consistency of the calligraphy and the semantics with the authenticity of the paper and ink is reasonably conclusive. You have a genuine, ancient document here."

"I could have told you that," grumbled the Duke.

Very impressive," beamed Ilsa. "Can I have that in a report?"

"Sure," said Sunil.

CHAPTER 20

TO PUBLISH, NOT PERISH

Ilsa approached the office of Dr. Dr. Bradford M. Bradford armed with her thesis. But she hesitated a moment before opening the outer door. Habit made her tremble before the awful majesty of the dean. Still, her recent adventures changed things. Had the dean ever hijacked a Spanish ship of the line? Run a British blockade at sea? Had he ever trudged over hill and dale to a Revolutionary army camp? Had he ever shaken hands with George Washington or flown a kite with Benjamin Franklin? Did he have an actual duke staying in his spare bedroom? She was pretty sure the dean would fail all these simple tests. Jutting out her chin, Ilsa banged open the outer door to Bradford's office suite, causing the sour secretary to make a vertical ascent about three feet toward the ceiling. Before the sour secretary could recover and protest, Ilsa barged past her into Bradford's inner sanctum. The dean looked up, scowling from under his black caterpillar eyebrows.

"I don't have you in my appointment book," he groused.

"No. But once I publish this," she said, plopping her thesis down on his desk, *"you* will need an appointment to see *me.*"

Bradford jerked suddenly straight. "Are you trying to be impertinent?" he asked.

"Oh, no," said Ilsa. "If I were trying, I would succeed."

The double Ph.D. was unaccustomed to such effrontery. His godlike position usually cowed his subordinates. Stymied, he simply asked, "How can I help you?"

"I have found the paradigm-shattering thesis you said I needed for tenure," replied Ilsa.

"Oh, have you?" said Bradford, acidly. "Well, I shall be the judge of that."

"Be my guest," said Ilsa, sitting down, uninvited.

Bradford frowned, but picked up the thesis, at first holding it as if he were touching something that should properly be handled only with tongs. As he made it past the second page, however, his eyes widened, as he sank hypnotically into his chair. He began flipping the pages frantically, breathing more and more stertorously. Beads of sweat began to pop on his domelike forehead. After reading the conclusion on the last page, he dropped the thesis on his blotter with a thud. When he first attempted speech, his vocal cords failed him. "The original document?" he asked when he finally found his voice.

With a triumphant smile, Ilsa spread the Almaviva Title Deed on his desk. "The original," she said. And, laying down beside it another file, she added, "Dr. Deshmukh's appraisal of authenticity."

Bradford's mouth gaped like a codfish. Ilsa enjoyed the awkward silence. How different from her last, timorous encounter with this man.

"But, my dear Dr. Guilford-Schlitz, this is, this is...?"

"I know," she said.

Suddenly the man of action, Bradford sprung for his telephone and barked at his sour secretary. "Get in here!"

The sour secretary whizzed in.

"Stop the university presses!"

"We don't have presses," said the sour secretary. "We publish online."

"It's just an expression. Give this to our staff and get it published right away. Put out a press release. And have the graphics department make a hi-res image of this document. Careful!"

The sour secretary, who had begun to reach for the document, cringed.

"It's a historical artifact," growled Bradford.

"Yes, sir," said the sour secretary, picking it up gingerly, along with the thesis, and backing out of the room.

"Dr. Dr. Bradford," Ilsa began.

"Brad," corrected the dean genially.

"Brad, then," said Ilsa. "What about my tenure?"

"Well," said Bradford, "It's not my decision alone, obviously, but I think in light of this astounding discovery, the board will find...."

"I'm sure they will," said Ilsa confidently. She stood up and resumed singing the *Publish or Perish tango.*

SONG: *PUBLISH OR PERISH*

Ilsa: You see, sir, I tried sir.

I searched far and wide, sir,

For a thesis that would take the world by storm.

I finally came through, sir,
(though no thanks to you, sir)
With a theory that is far outside the norm.

Overcome with enthusiasm, Bradford sprung out from behind his desk and began tangoing with Ilsa.

Both: Publish or perish, it's a thrilling dance,
That every academic gets to do.
You come up with something novel and you take a chance
That your theory or your thesis will come through.
The mystifying magic of the published word
Gives us such a satisfying win.

The sour secretary cracked open the door to give Bradford an update on works in progress but froze as she spied the dean once more dancing with Ilsa.

Bradford: With this, I think your tenure here will be assured and will make the donor dollars tumble in.

Ilsa: *Olé!*

The sour secretary discreetly closed the door and backed away, shaking her head. "How," she asked herself, "do some people get to be deans?"

CHAPTER 21

THE STAR CHAMBER

In a dark and secret chamber in the Capitol, the Chairman of the Select Capital Riot Committee, Aaron Sniff, the Ranking Member, Dizzy Haney, and D.C. District Court Judge Elton Hackney stared down at the plaintiff, Ray Almaviva, who was wearing an orange prison jumpsuit and handcuffs. His attorney, Larry Grayson, spoke.

"Are the handcuffs really necessary, Mr. Chairman? My client is not a flight risk."

"He appears to have disappeared quite entirely when the FBI first attempted his arrest," said Haney, snarling.

"But he is here today," protested Larry.

"Because he is handcuffed," said Sniff.

"Well, I must protest this proceeding. My client has not been charged and arrested; and he is being treated as if guilty without being tried."

"Mr. Grayson," hissed Haney, "the charge against your client is attempted overthrew of the United States government."

"With all due respect, Ranking Member..." said Grayson. "There is no evidence to indicate that my client attempted anything of the kind or that he could have done so even if he had wanted to. His presence here in handcuffs, Mr. Chairman, would appear to prove that."

"It proves nothing of the kind," said Dizzy. "You have heard of the saying, 'treason never prospers. The reason? If it prospers, none dare call it treason?'"

"We are surely not entertaining a charge of treason," said Larry. "Treason is punishable by...?"

"Death," said Sniff, who gestured at an aid to wheel a projector into the center of the room. "Here is the evidence," he sneered.

The aid turned down the lights in the room and snapped the projector on. The first footage was of Ray at the Capitol building on the day of the protest. It was edited with diabolical selectivity.

Agent Schweppes: Do you love your country?

Ray: I'm going into the Capitol.

Shot of Ray entering the Capitol.

Ray: "All right, I'm going in."

Shot of the "Q-Anon Shaman" shaking Ray's hand.

Cut to Monica Bingley's interview with Ray.

Monica: Is this Capitol riot a threat to our Constitution?

Ray: It's an assault on our democracy. It's a threat to our Constitution. Polling is broken. Elections are broken. The truth will be out. You know what Stalin said: it's not who votes that counts. It's who counts the votes. And what did Cicero say? The more laws, the less justice. No one on either side of the aisle has ever been really serious about election integrity. There will not be left here one stone upon another that will not be thrown down. In the history of the world, these things happen. A new Civil War? There could be one."

"I think we have seen enough," said Haney.

At a gesture from Sniff, the aid turned the projector off and turned on the lights.

"That's nothing like what I said!" protested Ray.

"That's not you in the video?" enquired Judge Hackney.

"It is, but it's not the whole video," said Ray.

"Mr. Chairman, Ms. Ranking Member, Your Honor, those clips are selectively edited and do not tell the whole truth."

"On the contrary, sir, your client has condemned himself out of his own mouth," said Sniff.

"What he has done strikes at the root of our system of government," snarled Dizzy Haney.

"He will be detained," said Judge Hackney, "for a prison sentence of four years pending trial."

"*Pending* trial?" exploded Larry. "This is not even a regular court of law, and you're putting him in jail *pending* trial?"

Hackney reached for the gavel, but Sniff got ahold of it first and hammered it down. "Take the prisoner away," said he.

"Who's undermining the Constitution now?" shouted Ray, as Federal agents hauled him off.

CHAPTER 22

PRECEDENT STRIKES BACK

Larry Grayson sat with Ilsa and the Duke in Ilsa's apartment. They had three cups of untouched, cold tea before them. Ilsa's cell phone buzzed, but she turned off the call.

"It's outrageous!" the Duke suddenly cried. "This America, this country I helped to found, it has become worse than all the royal tyrannies of Europe!"

Larry looked at Don Raimondo quizzically. "You helped to found?"

"He means, just as we all do, as voting citizens," said Ilsa, covering up for Don Raimondo nervously.

"I want to go to Congress and ask for my treasure back!" fumed the Duke.

"His treasure back?" asked Larry, turning to Ilsa even more puzzled. Ilsa shot a warning glance at the Duke, but it was lost on him. "He's very patriotic," she explained. "He doesn't think his tax dollars should be abused."

"Well, neither do I," said Larry. "I've never seen anything like this lawlessness. And I agree with you, sir; it's tyranny, and as bad as anything in history."

"I guarantee it," said Don Raimondo.

Ilsa's phone buzzed frantically again, but she continued to ignore the call.

"Even King George III would not have behaved like these scoundrels," growled Don Raimondo. "I can tell you that from personal experience."

"From....?" Larry's voice trailed off as he raised his eyebrows and looked to Ilsa for clarification.

"He's a keen student of history, as I am," said Ilsa, doing her best to avoid having to explain the presence in her apartment of an actual eighteenth-century duke.

"I see," said Larry. He leaned over to Ilsa and whispered, "Who is this guy again?"

"He's Ray's cousin. From Ohio," she said.

"How come he speaks with a Spanish accent?"

"He grew up in Miami."

"Miami, Ohio?

"Florida."

"Ah," said Larry. "Anyway, you wanted me to read something." Ilsa's phone buzzed hysterically again and again she rejected the call.

"Yes," she replied. "I had hoped you might have had the time to read it before Ray went before the Committee."

"What Committee?" said Larry with a mirthless laugh. "They didn't even have the guts to assemble the whole Committee. Just the Chairman, the Ranking Member, and a jumped-up D.C. District Court Judge."

"This is my article," said Ilsa, "just published under the auspices of my university. It's on the internet, and..." Her phone vibrated again, bouncing off the coffee table. "And my phone is exploding."

"Exploding? Why?" asked Larry.

"My thesis went live online while you were before the Committee, Larry. Let me spell it out."

And, spreading the Almaviva Title Deed on the coffee table, Ilsa told Larry the whole, astonishing saga, with Don Raimondo exclaiming, "Exactly!" and *"Por su puesto!"* at regular intervals. Larry's eyes widened to the size of silver dollars. It took him a moment after Ilsa had finished her discourse to find his voice. He coughed to check that his vocal chords still worked. "Is this true?" he asked.

"Completely!" thundered Don Raimondo.

Larry jumped up and paced around the room, his legal brain whirring. Then he stopped and took Ilsa squarely by her slender shoulders, gazing deeply into her soft, brown eyes. "It can't be true," he said firmly, struggling to get a grip on this improbable reality.

Ilsa's phone vibrated again, now tumbling across the floor like a small animal trying to escape.

"The document is authenticated," said Ilsa, picking up Sunil's report from the table. "And that's why my phone is blowing up." She bent down to pick up her phone to stop the buzzing. She glanced at the screen and held it out for Larry to inspect.

"Not only the American press, but the international press have picked up the story. Researchers in London, Paris, and Madrid have searched their national archives and dug up contemporary copies of this deed. It's real."

Larry stared for a moment into the middle distance, dazed. Coming back to earth, he delicately picked up the Almaviva Title Deed and, perusing the bottom of the page, said, "These signatures...John Adams, Thomas Jefferson, Benjamin Franklin, James Madison, Samuel Chase, and John Hancock...all Founders... all signatories to the Declaration of Independence."

"That's right," said Ilsa, "and notice the date."

Larry inspected the date: 1776. He thought for a moment and then let the deed fall from his nerveless fingers to the floor. "It predates the United States Constitution!"

"Exactly," said Ilsa. "So, it takes precedent over Article 1, Section 9, Clause 8...."

"Which says," cited Larry, snapping instantly back into the role of top student in law school, "'no title of nobility shall be granted by the United States.'"

"Exactly," said Ilsa in triumph.

"So," mused Larry, "since they had already made this character a duke, his title trumps the Constitution."

"Character?" repeated Don Raimondo, offended.

"Just a figure of speech," said Ilsa, soothing him.

"Which means," said Larry, "that Ray Almaviva is a real American *duke.*"

"Yes..." prompted Ilsa.

"And," continued Larry, working it all out aloud, "that he has legal title to all the land on which the District of Columbia now sits."

"Precisely," said Ilsa.

"And I want it back, now!" thundered Don Raimondo.

"He means we all do, in the interests of justice," said Ilsa quickly.

Ilsa's phone buzzed again. She switched it off again.

"Good God!" cried Larry. "So what do we do with this?"

"Well, you're the lawyer," said Ilsa.

"Yes," said Larry. "I suppose I am. OK, let me get my firm on this. My whole staff. We need to assert Ray's rights."

CHAPTER 23

WAKING THE
PRESIDENT

Chief of Staff Nelson McGaffer and Press Secretary Daisy Katrina Perdue edged cautiously into the Oval Office. They gestured silence to the Speaker of the House Fanny Villosi, the House Minority Leader, and Kenny McMurphy the Senate's Majority Leader, along with Jack Boomer, the Minority Leader of the Senate Fitch McCormack, and the Chief Justice of the Supreme Court John Windsock. McGaffer gestured for them to remain waiting for a moment in the hall.

President Beau Haydn was bent over the Resolute desk, snoring gently with the tip of his nose submerged in a half-eaten bowl of rice pudding.

"Should we wake him?" asked Daisy.

"We usually try not to," said Nelson.

"But this is an emergency. At least a publicity emergency," said Daisy.

"All right," sighed McGaffer. He walked over to the desk and shook the President lightly by the shoulder. "Mr. President...Mr. President..."

The Leader of the Free World slowly regained consciousness and sat up, a dab of rice pudding adorning the tip of his nose. "It's great to be in Pennsylvania," he said. "You know, I got hairy legs that turn blond in the sun. And the kids used to come up and reach in the pool, rub my leg down so it was straight and then watch the hair come back up again. So, I learned about roaches.... I learned about kids jumping on my lap. Oh, how I love kids jumping on my lap."

Nelson and Daisy exchanged painful glances.

"Uh, Mr. President, maybe you're not getting enough sleep," said Daisy in a kindly tone.

The President looked at her befogged for a moment. Then he recognized her.

"Oh, hello, Daisy. What? Oh, you may be right. Yesterday I only got four hours of sleep."

"Well, that's not enough," she said compassionately.

"And the day before," said the President, "I got three hours."

"Well, there you go," said Daisy.

"And the day before that, I only slept for two hours."

"Mr. President, to be in good health, you need to get more sleep at night."

"Oh, at night?" said the President. "At night, I get eight hours."

Nelson and Daisy exchanged uneasy glances again. Neither had the courage to wipe the smudge of rice pudding from the presidential beak. Impatient of waiting, the congressional delegation and the Chief Justice slithered into the room.

"Mr. President," said Speaker Villosi, "we have a problem."

"Oh," said the President, grinning.

"Not a funny one," said Speaker Villosi.

"Oh," said the President, frowning.

McGaffer took over. "As you know, sir, we have arrested a lot of people involved in the outrageous insurrection attempt at the Capitol."

"How many?" asked the President.

"A few hundred," said Speaker Villosi. "Maybe a thousand."

"Good! Too many people think the ends justify the means. They should all be shot!" said the President.

"Not without a proper trial," exclaimed Congressman McMurphy. "Outrageous!"

"What's outrageous," said Senator Boomer, turning purple, "is this assault on our democracy."

"I tend to agree," drawled Senator McCormack.

"Can we please focus on informing the President of the matter at hand?" said McGaffer impatiently.

A gentle snoring wafted over the Resolute desk and resonated in the acoustically vibrant Oval Office. President Haydn had resumed his nap with his nose again dipping into his rice pudding. The delegation of officials rolled their eyes.

"Mr. President," said Daisy, rubbing his shoulder sympathetically.

"Ah!" said the President, jerking alert. "It's great to be in Ohio!"

"Mr. President," said McGaffer sternly. "The problem is about one of the people we put in jail. We need to show you a news item. Daisy...?"

The Press Secretary took a remote control and pressed a button. A recording of Monica Bingley's TV show flickered on. She was interviewing Ilsa, Larry, and Bradford.

"So, Dr. Guilford-Schlitz, it turns out that Ray Almaviva is actually a real-life American duke and owns half of Washington, D.C.?"

"Not half. All of it," said Larry.

"And because the whole thing was written up by the Founding Fathers...," said Monica.

"It has the force of law," said Larry.

"So this is like a separate country inside the United States?" asked Monica.

"Exactly!" beamed Ilsa.

"And it all checks out?" Monica asked.

"Absolutely," said Bradford before Monica could reply. And he put a cozy hand on Ilsa's sleeve. "She's my star researcher. Our university is proud of her."

Daisy snapped the gruesome broadcast off. The whole delegation stared at the President, awaiting his take. He was dozing again. Daisy shook his shoulder, and he shuddered awake. "It's great to be in Illinois," he announced.

"Mr. President," said Chief Justice Windsock, "perhaps you haven't grasped the gravity of the situation. Congress arrested this guy, thinking to make him pay his debt to society. Well, it turns out society may owe him a lot more than he owes to it."

"How much?" asked Haydn.

"Too much," said Windsock.

"Can we pay him with the pandemic slush fund?" asked Haydn. "We've paid for so much with that slush fund. We even used it," he said smiling nostalgically, "to set up my Center for Diplomacy and Global Engagement."

"It's not enough," said Speaker Villosi.

"We owe him that much?" asked Haydn.

"I'm afraid we might," said the Speaker of the House.

"So what should we do?" asked the President.

"You have to talk to him," said Senator Boomer.

"Why me?" asked the President.

"Because you're head of state," said Speaker Villosi, "I don't know quite how to put this, but...."

"He's also a head of state," said Windsock, flatly.

There was a moment of grim silence. No one had yet quite dared to put it that way, but there it was, the elephant in the room.

"Look," said McGaffer, "we've written out everything you need to say on these three-by-five cards."

"OK," said President Haydn. He took them and began to shuffle and deal them across his desk.

"Better use the teleprompter," whispered Daisy to McGaffer.

CHAPTER 24

THE PRISONER AND THE PRESIDENT

Two prison guards escorted Ray down a gray corridor in orange jail clothes. From their cells, the other prisoners watched him balefully. Everyone in this cell block had been arrested on charges of insurrection, and they shuddered. *"Illegitimi non carborundum!"* cried one of the inmates, a scholarly type with thick glasses.

One of the guards halted in his tracks. He walked over to the scholarly gentleman's cell. "What did you say?" he asked.

"It's Latin," said Ray. "It means don't let the bastards grind you down."

"Who you calling a bastard?" snarled the guard, pushing his face up against the bars of the scholarly gentleman's cell.

"Let him be," said the other guard. "His turn is coming." The guards exchanged a wicked smile and resumed escorting Ray on his perp walk.

In his office, the Warden, a fat, sweating official, paced nervously back and forth in front of Larry Grayson, Ray's lawyer.

"Is he really a...?"

"You saw it on Monica Bingley's show," said Larry.

The Warden stopped in his tracks, awed. "Then it must be true!" After a moment's reflection, he approached Larry confidentially and asked, "What's the proper form of address?"

"Huh?"

The Warden rubbed his pudgy hands. "I've had a lot of celebrities in my jail, but I never met a dook before. What do I call him? Yer Honor?"

"Uh...I think it's...uh... 'Your Grace.'"

The Warden's eyes widened. "Your Grace? Your Grace!" He paced around, practicing. "Good afternoon, Your Grace. Of course, Your Grace. By all means, Your Grace."

The guards rolled into the Warden's office with Ray, handcuffed, in tow. Larry leaped to his feet. Ray brightened. "Larry!"

"Ray!" cried Larry. "I raised your bail!"

"How?" asked Ray. "The bail was a million dollars."

Deadpan, Larry replied, "I mortgaged Georgetown."

Ray's mind boggled.

"Guards!" cried the Warden, indignantly. "Release His Grace!"

"Whose Grace?" asked one of the guards, baffled.

"His Grace," said the Warden, pointing at Ray.

"My Grace," affirmed Ray.

The guard was still confused.

"The prisoner, you dolt!" barked the Warden. Bowing to Ray, he added, "I'm sorry, Your Grace."

Just then, the desk phone jangled. The Warden picked it up, in irritation at first, but as he listened, he stiffened slowly to attention, began to sweat even more profusely, and stammered. "Hamana-hamana-hamana-hama..." The Warden covered the telephone mouthpiece and turned to Ray. "It's for Your Grace," he said in a strangled voice.

"For me?" Ray asked. "Who is it?"

"The...the President of the United States," croaked the Warden.

"Very funny. Are we free to go?"

The Warden passed the phone like a hot potato. "It's really.... him!"

Ray stared quizzically at Larry, then took the receiver. "Hello?" he said gingerly.

"Hello, Ray," came a warm voice. "This is Bo Haydn. I'm happy to be in California."

"Read the teleprompter!" came a harsh whisper from the President's side of the connection.

"What?" said Ray.

"It's Beau Haydn." The President paused for effect.

"Beau Haydn?" asked Ray. "The President of the United States?"

"He's asking if I'm the President," whispered Beau Haydn to his Press Secretary.

"Well, tell him yes!" she whispered back.

"OK," he said, "Yes, Ray. I'm the President."

Ray considered this information. He held his arm out and looked at his orange prison shirt, reflecting. His gorge rose. "You're really the President?" he asked.

In the Oval Office, Haydn glanced confusedly at Daisy. This was not going exactly according to the script. "Of the United States. Yes. I know you're impressed, but..."

"Wait a minute!" interrupted Ray testily. "I think we should settle a point of protocol, don't you?"

"What?" asked Haydn.

"Since we're both heads of state," continued Ray, "should I call you Beau, and you call me Ray, or should I call you Mr. President, and you call me Your Grace?"

The Warden, aghast, sank feebly into his chair.

"What!" snapped Haydn.

Ray handed Larry the phone.

"You're my lawyer," said Ray in a bored tone. "You talk to him."

For a moment, Larry was stunned. Then he raised the phone to his lips and gulped. "Uh...sir...?"

CHAPTER 25

THE BRAIN TRUST

Chief of Staff Nelson McGaffer, Press Secretary Daisy Katrina-Perdue, Speaker of the House Fanny Villosi, House Minority Leader Kenny McMurphy, Majority Leader of the Senate Jack Boomer, Minority Leader of the Senate Fitch McCormack, and Chief Justice of the Supreme Court John Windsock all stood around the Oval Office as President Beau Haydn hung up the phone. With a benign smile, he asked, "How'd I do?"

Ignoring the President, Speaker Villosi turned to McGaffer and growled, "Another fine mess you've got us into."

"Me?" said McGaffer, affronted. "You're the one who had the Capitol Police let the protestors inside the building!"

"Well, you're the one who had the FBI inciting the crowd!" retorted Fanny.

"And you're the one who's suppressing all the security camera footage!" said Daisy Katrina-Perdue to Fanny.

"And you're the one who ran this duffer's campaign from his

basement and rigged the election," said Congressman McMurphy to McGaffer.

"I am not going to stand here and listen to that Big Lie!" shouted Senator Jack Boomer.

"Well, stand somewhere else, if you like, but if you hang around me, you're going to hear it," said Congressman McMurphy, who was the Leader of the Opposition in the House.

"I think we need to take these allegations of insurrection seriously," said Senator McCormack, who was the Leader of the Opposition in the Senate.

"I understand you all want to cover your tracks, but the eight-hundred-pound orangutan in the room is the legal validity of this so-called Almaviva Title Deed," said Chief Justice Windsock.

"I can get the press, social media, and Big Tech to smear it and bury it," said Daisy, happy to be of help.

"I can hold a Congressional press conference and debunk it," said Speaker Villosi.

"But this thing has gone international," said McGaffer. "What are the full, legal implications?"

Chief Justice John Windsock gripped the lapels of his coat, cleared his throat authoritatively, and gazed at the ceiling as if he were a cop giving testimony in traffic court. "Well," he began, "in the first place if validated, this document was signed by several of the most prominent Founders and signatories of the Declaration of Independence. Since it predates the Constitution, it is more than constitutional. It is super-constitutional."

"Meaning?" asked Senator McCormack.

"Meaning," continued Windsock, "it would have authority transcending the Constitution. As such, it would be a valid exception to Article 1, Section 9, Clause 8, which says..." He again cleared his throat officially. "'No title of nobility shall be granted by the United States.'"

"And what effect does that have?" asked Senator Boomer.

"Nothing in particular by itself, but in conjunction with his territorial rights...."

"Are you taking that seriously?" asked McGaffer.

"You went to law school. The Fifth Amendment, I need hardly remind you," said Windsock, "says that 'no person shall be deprived of life, liberty, or property without due process of law.'"

"And so?" asked the Senator.

"And so," said the Chief Justice gravely, "the very ground on which we now stand may be his, not ours."

"The White House?" gasped McGaffer.

"And the Supreme Court," said the Chief Justice, choking back a sob.

"Oh, that would be too rich," laughed Congressman McMurphy. "I can just see sheriffs hurrying all nine Justices in silly black robes out the back door of the Court!"

Windsock bristled. "You might find it less droll when those same sheriffs escort all 435 Congressmen and one hundred Senators down the Capitol steps."

"You mean...?" gasped Senator Boomer.

"Yes, I mean the Capitol you are claiming he violated may be sitting illegally on his property," said Windsock.

"Well, let's seize his property!" cried McGaffer. "The national interest! Eminent domain!"

"You're forgetting the second part of the Fifth Amendment: 'Nor shall private property be taken for public use, without just compensation.' You can hardly blame the Capitol rioters for undermining the Constitution unless you are prepared to uphold it."

"Well," said Speaker Villosi in desperation, "can we fast-track this Title Deed to the Supreme Court and get it debunked?"

Chief Justice Windsock winced. "We can fast-track it to the Court, but, as you know, the decisions of the Justices are never easy to predict, even by the Chief Justice."

"Especially by the Chief Justice," grumbled Senator Boomer.

"The Justices will ask questions," said Windsock, "and then their clerks will write opinions which they will sign. In a case of this importance, the Justices might even read their opinions before signing them. It will be the landmark case of all landmark cases. So, the outcome will depend strictly on the evidence."

"For once," murmured Congressman McMurphy.

"Well, let's manufacture the evidence!" cried Speaker Villosi. "The fate of the Federal City hangs in the balance."

"I'm afraid it's worse than that," said the Chief Justice.

"How could it be worse?" asked Daisy with childlike curiosity.

"Well," drawled Windsock, "this person, this Ray Almaviva, is not just a property owner because, you see, the property was deemed a duchy by the Founders before the official formation of the United States as a country. That means the Duchy of Almaviva is, so to speak, a country within our country, and the man was probably correct legally in referring to himself as a head of state."

"So, the Duchy would be kind of like the Vatican City—an independent state in the heart of Rome," ventured Congressman McMurphy.

"Like that, but worse," said Windsock. "Because the Vatican is a state within the city of Rome. The District of Columbia is a city entirely within the Duchy of Almaviva."

The room lapsed into a moment of stunned silence.

"All right," said McGaffer grimly, "Let's get to work. Fanny, Jack, you search the Library of Congress for evidence that this deed is fake. Mr. President, we'll call the State Department and the CIA to conduct opposition research."

The President's attention had wandered back to his half-eaten bowl of rice pudding, which had begun again to sample. "Check," said the President without looking up. "Shall I call them now?"

"Not now, sir. We'll get you a script," said McGaffer.

"On it," chirped Daisy Katrina-Perdue.

"John, you confer with your fellow Justices," said McGaffer. The Chief Justice nodded. "All right, everyone!" shouted McGaffer clapping his hands. "Let's get moving!"

Everyone scuttled out of the Oval Office except the President. He sat for a moment, musing. Then he began talking to himself. "They all think they're so smart. No, no, no, no, no. They don't get it. If you show you're all thumbs, you'll never have to lift a finger. I'm the President. I take all the perks. Let them do all the work." And clenching his right fist, he wobbled to his feet and declared, "I have the power." He walked into the middle of the Oval Office and, with a surprising agility in private that he never manifested in public, he burst into a song and dance.

SONG: *TOO BAD TO BE TRUE*

President: Oh, I'm the President, with power
To drone the Eiffel Tower
And make those surly Frenchies all cry, *"Sacre bleu!"*
I can sap a generation
With taxes and inflation
That recklessly exceed the nation's revenue.
I can set Russia back
With a pipeline attack,
Oh, man, I'm too bad to be true!

I name ambassadors and judges
To settle scores and grudges
And thank them for their little gifts
Of campaign cash.
By executive disorder
I can open up the border
Giving Florida and Texas a new voting class.
I'm always pleased to appease
The Red Chinese,
Oh, man, I'm such a pain in the...
[Spoken] Well, let's keep it family friendly...
[Sung] Neck!

I can pardon any treason
Without a rhyme or reason,
And nobody is free to even disagree.
And I don't care who hollers,
I take taxpayer dollars,
And use them to support my favorite nominee—
Guess who?
And if you'd care for World War Three,
Just leave that up to me!
Oh, yeah, leave *that* up to me!

Haydn threw a little sand on the Oval Office floor and performed a soft shoe dance to six bars, much to his own satisfaction. He finished with a rousing refrain in the seventh, final bar.

President: You can leave that up to me!

Content but exhausted, Haydn plopped back into the presidential chair. In a trice, he nodded off, the tip of his nose again submerging gently into the still-unfinished bowl of rice pudding.

CHAPTER 26

THE SUPREME COURT DECIDES

Chief Justice John Windsock sat in his study surrounded by a mountain of documents. He was within easy reach of a decanter of thirty-year-old single malt Scotch, one bottle of a crate he had received, by strange coincidence, after casting a telling vote on a tricky case regarding pharmaceutical price controls. He was facing what was perhaps the most difficult decision in the history of the Supreme Court. As his cursed luck would have it, his would be the deciding vote. Four Justices had voted against honoring the Almaviva Title Deed, and four Justices had voted for it.

The authenticity of the document was not in question. Authorities from all over the world had now validated it. The question was whether the Duchy of Almaviva was a legitimate, independent state and whether the United States had illegitimately usurped its authority. He picked up one of the documents on his desk and read it with distaste. Why was Congress always so sloppy?

On July 9, 1790, Congress passed the Residence Act, approving the creation of a national capital on the Potomac River, but they did not specify a location. They left that decision to George Washington, who, as a surveyor, significantly mapped out the city of Alexandria in Virginia, which, as things turned out, the District of Columbia did not include. So they intentionally or otherwise "forgot" about the original plan of including part of Virginia in the Federal City. But how could they forget about the Almaviva Title Deed when they established the District on the north bank of the Potomac River in 1791? Was it because the Duke had gone to France to witness the signing of the Treaty of Paris, ending the war with Britain, in 1783? Was it because he had never returned to America? Was he out of sight, out of mind? Or did they think that when he joined the French Revolution in 1789, that he had abandoned his claim? Did they think they could just get away with sweeping it all under the rug? Well, thought the Chief Justice with a sigh, it wouldn't be the first time. After all, it was the Continental Congress that endorsed the deed; it was the second Congress of the United States that passed the Residence Act and the sixth Congress that held its first session in the District of Columbia. Those successive Congresses might have forgotten about it. But surely George Washington wouldn't have forgotten about it. Or maybe there was a shady deal. Perhaps that was why, despite the original plan, the District of Columbia never claimed any part of Virginia or any part of George Washington's private land.

Whatever happened, it was clear what didn't happen. The Federal government did not honor its agreement with the Duke of Almaviva; they just stepped on it and built their capital city where the Duchy was supposed to be. And there was no compensation paid to the Duke or to his descendants, so there was no defense of eminent domain. And speaking of descendants, all the authorities had also proven that this Ray Almaviva bozo was indeed a descendant of the original Don Raimondo de Borbón y Cortés, Count of Almaviva and former Governor of His Most Catholic Majesty's colony, Santa Cecilia. So, there was a *bona fide* American duke alive and kicking today.

Windsock picked up a blue-covered brief. Ray's lawyer was arguing that since the Title Deed of Almaviva was signed by the Founders twelve years before the creation of the U.S. Constitution, it had equal, if not more, authority than the Constitution. The lawyers were now throwing around terms like "pre-constitutional" and "super-constitutional." Whatever all that meant, Windsock knew this much: the document was not *un*constitutional, and constitutionality was what the Supreme Court was created to judge.

Whether the Duchy could act independently of the United States due to prior rights or whether the United States could exercise authority over the Duchy due to the long course of dealing was something he did not feel competent to decide. The Continental Congress had created this mess, the U.S. Congress and the first President had ignored it, and it was really up to the current U.S. Congress and the current President to fix it. All he could say was that the Duke's claims were based on authenticated documents and warranties which were not unconstitutional. And there was no precedent to fall back on. It wasn't a Solomonic decision, but it was all he could really say. So, with a great sigh and another swig of his excellent Scotch, he began writing his opinion. The next day, that screed rocked the world.

CHAPTER 27

DUTY FREE

Winter's last grip on nature was beginning to wither. Spring, although not yet here, was leaving faint hints of its floral promise in the air. On the street in front of Ray's apartment, there was a gaggle of journalists and satellite trucks, empurpling the otherwise pleasant air with on-camera monologues and cigarette smoke. And despite the benevolent weather, the atmosphere inside was overcast.

Ray sank into his sofa with a fifth of Scotch in one hand and a crystal tumbler in the other. The bottle was but one-third full. Don Raimondo was in the kitchen, tinkering with appliances. He was endlessly fascinated with the inventions of the twenty-first century, and he was forever taking them apart—and breaking them. Ray was annoyed at the sound of the refrigerator door opening and closing, opening and closing.

"Yes," hollered Ray, "the light goes off when the door is closed."

"Ah!" said the Duke.

True, Ray was free, but getting unjustly arrested had ruined his mood. Much as he liked his esteemed ancestor, the original Duke, he wondered how long he would need to put up with nobility in his spare bedroom. It also bothered him that Don Raimondo had spent several nights in Ilsa's spare bedroom. It was irksome to imagine this jumped-up grandee from over two centuries ago, someone who was old enough to be her great-great-great-great grandfather (however many greats there actually were in there), standing whenever she entered a room, pulling out chairs for her, endlessly kissing her hand, and who knows what else? What made it worse was that Ray and Don Raimondo were family. It bordered on the indecent.

Don Raimondo simply had to go back. If he didn't get back to the past, Ray's ancestors would never be born, and thus Ray would never be born. No wonder he was in a bad mood! And he was annoyed at the journalists and the worldwide publicity. He couldn't go back to teaching because every time he stepped outside, he was mobbed. He had tenure, so he was still getting paid, but he was restless—no, not restless, cranky. Perhaps it was too much to call him disgruntled, but he was far from gruntled. His whole life before had been *laissez-faire*—live and let live. And now here he was, personally, the eye of a political hurricane. Probably, for once in his life, he should take sides, but the problem was, whether it was one wall of the hurricane or the other, either side was still a hurricane. Nothing made sense, and it was all Ilsa's fault.

Just then, Larry and Ilsa bobbed through the front door, shouting ecstatically. "Here it is!" cried Larry. He handed Ray a printed, blue-covered brief.

"The decision of the Supreme Court!" squealed Ilsa. "It validates all my research!"

"Well, bully for you," said Ray sourly.

"Well, it also validates your Title Deed," said Ilsa, ice entering her tone.

"Well," said Larry, "to be precise, it doesn't invalidate it, which is about as good as a Supreme Court decision gets."

Sounds of a disturbance outside were growing. Ilsa pulled a curtain aside and looked out the window.

"Larry, Come here!" she cried.

"What?"

"Outside!"

Larry dashed to the window. Then he and Ilsa flung open the front door. Ray wearily rose from his sofa, cradling his tumbler and bottle of Scotch, and followed them, with Don Raimondo coming after him. At Ray's appearance, a gaggle of journalists pounced, yelling questions and thrusting microphones into his face. Squinting in the sunlight, Ray followed Ilsa's trembling finger to a traffic jam at the end of the street. There was angry honking. A hostile crowd was milling around a gas station.

"What's going on?" asked Larry.

"Let's go see," said the ever-reckless Ilsa.

She, Larry, and Don Raimondo bounded off. Sighing, Ray put down his glass and decanter and followed, elbowing his way past the mob of reporters who nipped at him like famished piranhas. At the far end of the street was a gas station, whose owner was trying to placate angry motorists.

"I'm sorry, sir," said the owner. "It's all gone."

"It's rationing!" thundered one of the motorists.

"It's not fair!" shouted another.

"I'm stayin' right here till I get my gas!" cried a third.

The gas station owner turned to Ilsa and said, "It's a riot!"

"Not another one," groused Ray.

Larry looked at the gas pump. The posted prices were:

Regular: $1.659/gallon
Unleaded: $1.719/gallon
High-Octane: $1.799/gallon.

Larry smiled at the owner. "Well, no wonder. You're giving it away."

"I'm not," protested the owner.

"Well, who is?" asked Larry.

"The oil company," said the owner. "They came to fill me up this morning and reset all the pumps."

"At those prices?" asked Ray. "It used to be over three bucks."

"That's right," said the owner. "They said with all this Dooky of Albuquerque stuff, there's no tax on gas."

"What?" blurted Larry.

"They said we're outside America or something."

"You mean just the tax part of gas used to be...over a dollar?" asked Ray.

"Guess so," said the gas station owner. "When folks found out, they came round and pumped me dry."

"You must be going broke," said Larry, "selling gas this low."

"Naw," said the owner. "I still make the same as I did before. Only I don't owe no tax on it."

"Is it legal?" gulped Larry.

"I dunno," said Ilsa. "You're the lawyer."

Don Raimondo, fascinated, was fiddling with the gas pump.

"Stop that," said Ray, annoyed.

CHAPTER 28

TAX HAVEN

Later that day, an attorney in an ostentatiously expensive suit made his way through the mob of reporters and up the steps of Ray's apartment building. Just as he was about to enter, two men from a slick ad agency, carrying large, black art portfolios, barged past him with all the patience of housewives at a deli counter. The attorney stood aside but followed them into Ray's apartment.

"Have we caught yer Nobleness at a good time?" asked the first ad man of Ray.

"What is all this?" asked Ray.

"Allow me to introduce myself. I'm Bob Herringbone from the ad agency of Grogan, Herringbone, Wackenhut, and Weeks."

"And this is Dick Grogan," said Herringbone.

"It's a pleasure," grinned Grogan, in a gravelly voice suggestive of someone who had dunked many a society offender into the East River.

"We got two very exciting proposals, yer Excellency. Tell him, Grogan."

Grogan and Herringbone quickly set up two easels and balanced artwork upon them, one poster showing a new model Cadillac, the other a blue-white can of cola. Standing back for a moment to admire their work, they took a deep breath and wound up for the pitch. Before Ray could interject, the boys bubbled over.

"Yer gonna love this, Yer Greatness," said Grogan with a juicy grin. "Cadillac wants to bring out a new model, and they're calling it...."

"Are you ready?" enquired Herringbone, leaping from one foot to the other.

Grogan, the human semaphore, declared: "The American Duke!"

"Classy?" asked Herringbone. "Classy!" affirmed Herringbone. "And, oh! Oh! Tell him the other one!"

Grogan made a grotesque pirouette. "A new soft drink, yer Majesty, called—get this—Ducal Cola!"

"It's Coke with a touch of class...," said Herringbone.

"In a blue can!" added Grogan.

"Blue blood, blue can. Get it?" said Herringbone.

"Whaddya say?" rasped Grogan, spreading a contract out on Ray's coffee table and holding an uncapped fountain pen above its dotted line.

"Uh...," said Ray.

"What can ya say?" exclaimed Herringbone.

"You gotta use this title of yours, dook," said Grogan, slapping Ray's back.

"While it's hot," said Herringbone, poking Ray in the ribs.

"It's called branding," said Grogan.

"Getting something for nothing but who you are and who you know," said Herringbone.

"We got the social media platforms all lit up, with sponsorships," said Grogan, "and we've already got you ten million followers ready to launch. Yer set for life, dook."

Larry cleared his throat. "We'd like to read the contract."

"Sure, sure, take yer time," said Grogan. "But remember, fifteen minutes of fame can pay for a lifetime of ease, but fifteen minutes can go by awful fast." Sidling up to Ray and winking, he added, "These endorsements are gonna make us—"

"Make you—" corrected Herringbone, bowing obsequiously to Ray.

"You," agreed Grogan. "Are gonna make you a fortune, yer Lordship."

"And nobody can work you better angles," said Herringbone, "than Grogan, Herringbone, Wackenhut—"

"And Weeks," added Grogan.

"We'll leave you with the artwork," said Herringbone.

"And call you in the morning," said Grogan. He made an imaginary pistol of his right hand, cocked it at His Grace, the Duke of Almaviva, and shot him a lascivious wink. The paragons of publicity bowed and backed out of the ducal presence in a manner they assumed to be the correct protocol in a palace.

The attorney in the ostentatiously expensive suit, who had been waiting forgotten and unobserved, now cleared his throat. "Ahem."

"Ah, yes," said Larry. "You were?"

"My card," said the attorney.

Larry took it and read: "Phil DeLuca."

"Senior Vice President and General Counsel to Consolidated Electric, Inc.," said Phil.

"Are you a lawyer?" asked Ilsa.

"May I draw your attention to the slogan on my card?"

"'Everything's a problem,'" read Ilsa.

"Yeah, he's a lawyer," confirmed Larry.

"Consolidated Electric has a proposal for you, Your Grace."

"Shoot," said Ray.

"As one of the largest corporations in the world, CE pays half a billion dollars annually in taxes. We don't like that."

Ray whistled.

"I wouldn't like it, either," said Larry.

"We've done a little legal research," continued Phil. "And the decision of the Supreme Court is good enough for us. The Duchy of Almaviva predates the American Republic. It has never signed any trade agreements with the United States, and the Almavivan people have never sent a representative to Congress. In America," said Phil, "you can't have taxation without representation."

"I'm not crazy about it, even with representation," said Ray.

"The point is," continued Phil, "You're not really in America."

"You mean...?" said Ilsa.

"No Federal tax, no sales tax, no American laws," said Phil.

"For everyone who lives in this neighborhood, right?" said Ray. "That's what was going on at the gas station this morning."

"Beyond that," said Phil in carefully measured tones. "Your Grace technically is the only citizen of the Duchy. But you have the authority to issue passports."

Ray pondered this for a moment. Then his eyes bulged, and he snapped his fingers. "So I could free everyone in this neighborhood from the burden of taxes?" asked Ray. His heart began to rumba. Getting back at the awful Federal government that had wrongfully imprisoned him was delicious. "All I have to do is issue them passports?"

"Ray," said Phil, "you could free everyone in America, if you felt like it."

There was a moment of numb silence as everybody in the room marinated in this idea. Gradually, a grin widened under Ray's Don Ameche mustache, and he breathed: "Wow!"

"But I'm not here about everyone in America," said Phil. "I'm here for Consolidated Electric. We want to set up our new corporate headquarters right here. Right now."

"Where?" asked Larry. "In his spare bedroom?"

"I'm staying there," objected Don Raimondo.

"Just a post office box," said Phil, in a bored, off-hand way. "That's all we need. But officially, we would be here. Exempt from Federal taxes. And," he inspected his expensive manicure, "we'll give you ten percent of everything we save."

"Good Lord, Ray!" cried Larry. "That's over fifty million dollars!"

"Paid quarterly," murmured Phil. "Is it a deal?"

"Monthly," countered Larry.

"Fine," said Phil.

Ray turned slowly and looked at Ilsa. Somehow, she had changed in his eyes. She was no longer Ilsa, the human pest, Ilsa, the reckless kook. She no longer put him in a bad mood. There was something about her that was almost prophetic. He wouldn't go so far as to say a halo was glowing around her auburn hair, but he couldn't positively swear that there wasn't.

Not long after, in the presidential limo, Nelson McGaffer glanced at his cell phone, startled at a headline, and pulled out a handkerchief to mop his dew-bespangled brow. He handed the phone to President Haydn, who stared at it momentarily before comprehending. Then he looked in astonishment at his Chief of Staff.

"He's doing what?" quivered the President.

McGaffer shifted uncomfortably. "He's stealing our tax base, sir."

"Whose tax base?" asked Haydn.

"The tax base," gurgled McGaffer, "of the entire United States!"

CHAPTER 29

CHANGE OF HEART

Ray sat on his sofa, lost in thought. Ilsa, Larry, and Don Raimondo were buzzing around the kitchen, swigging champagne and cheerfully preparing dinner. Don Raimondo, it turned out, was something of a gourmet chef. He would be, of course, thought Ray, annoyed. Ilsa was giggling and complimenting him on his many talents: hijacking the King's Treasure Fleet, commandeering an eighteenth-century battleship, nearly sinking a frigate of His Majesty's Royal Navy, funding the American Revolution, acquiring the title of duke, and now pulling out chairs, kissing hands, and preparing *paella de mariscos* from scratch. Ray liked Don Raimondo, but he thought it was only fair that ancestors should confine themselves to portraits in the family gallery and not barge into their descendants' lives. Then he had an idea.

"Larry," he said, "Why don't you take Don Raimondo out on the town?"

"And miss his *paella de mariscos?*" said Larry. "No way!"

Ray got up and went over to Larry. He took the champagne glass out of his hand, set it down, and pulled Larry aside.

"What's got into you?" asked Larry. "You should be celebrating with the rest of us. You're rich. You're wealthy. You're socially secure."

"Look," said Ray in a confidential, husky voice. "I need to get something straightened out."

"What?" asked Larry.

"It's private," said Ray.

"Well, I'm your lawyer. Your conversations with me are privileged and confidential."

"More private than that," said Ray. "I have to talk to Ilsa alone."

"Ah," said Larry, smiling. *"Amor."*

Ray bristled. "No, it's not *amor*, you idiot. It's just that we're all tangled up in this thing together, and I have to have a conversation with her alone. Can you get the Duke out of the way?"

"Well, I don't think I'm going to get him to abandon his *paella de mariscos,"* said Larry, glancing over at the Duke and Ilsa, who were chattering happily over the cutting board. "But maybe I can get him away for a few minutes."

"OK," said Ray. "Do it."

Larry went back into the kitchen. He looked at the almost empty bottle of champagne. "You know, Raimondo," he said, "I think we should not insult your *paella* by pairing it with the wrong wine."

"You are quite right," said the Duke. "We should pair it with something light, crisp, like a chilled *albariño."*

"Hey, Ray," called Larry, "Do we have any chilled *albariño?"*

"No, Larry, we don't," said Ray.

"Well, this won't do! C'mon, Raimondo, let's pop over to the wine shop and get some."

"But I'm cooking," said Don Raimondo.

"We'll just be a few minutes, and you're the best one to choose the correct Spanish wine."

"That's true," agreed Don Raimondo. "All right. Ilsa, my dear," he said, "keep an eye on the rice until I return." And he quite unnecessarily kissed her hand. It made Ray sick.

Of course, Larry and Don Raimondo had to battle the mob of reporters who never left Ray's stoop as they emerged onto the street, but Don Raimondo, in his swashbuckling way, plowed through them like Moses parting the Red Sea.

Ray wandered into the kitchen with feigned nonchalance. "Is there any more of that champagne left?" he asked Ilsa.

"Some," she said curtly, chopping onions. Ray picked up the bottle and turned it upside down over a flute. It yielded scarcely a drop. He frowned. The sound of Ilsa's chopping sounded distinctly hostile, like the war drums of some cannibal tribe.

"Would you stop that?" he asked.

"I'm done anyway," she said, putting down the knife and wiping her hands.

"Look," said Ray, "I don't know how long they're going to be gone, but..." He trailed off.

"Yes?" she asked.

"Well, I mean, I was pretty upset at all the mix-ups you got me into...."

"I got you into?" she said coolly. "It isn't my ancestor who became a duke."

"I know, I know. That's what I'm trying to say. I mean, it's not all your fault."

"No?" she said. "You mean it's not my fault that I got you out of jail and supplied the documents that won you a ruling in the Supreme Court and made you the owner of the District of Columbia and got you the title of a duke and fifty million dollars per year?"

"No, that is your fault," said Ray, "I mean, it's not your fault, but it's because of you that, well, all that stuff happened."

"Oh, thank you, Your Grace."

"Oh, don't call me that. I know you don't mean it."

"I'm sorry, Your Grace. Perhaps if I curtsey, it will seem more sincere." And she made an elaborate curtsey.

"Ilsa, cut it out! I just wanted to take you out on a date, and then all this craziness happened, and I'm a little confused."

He stared at her with puppy dog eyes. She contemplated his long lashes. No man should have lashes that long. It really wasn't fair. She almost melted. But then she remembered how rude he had been for so many days, well, centuries, actually, and how courtly and nice Don Raimondo had been.

"Well, I was confused when you asked me out, but I'm not anymore," said Ilsa.

"You're not?" asked Ray, feeling a glimmer of hope.

"No, I'm not," said Ilsa petulantly. "When I see Don Raimondo opening doors for me, and standing whenever I enter a room, and offering me a chair—"

"And kissing your hand," added Ray, bitterly.

"Well, yes," said Ilsa, "since you mention it, kissing my hand. Now I see what a real gentleman is like, and seeing what I might have settled for, I think I've had a very lucky escape."

"Oh, you do, do you?" said Ray.

"Yes, I do."

"So you liked Don Raimondo sleeping in your spare bedroom?"

"What are you saying?" seethed Ilsa.

"Or didn't he sleep in the *spare* bedroom?" asked Ray pointedly.

"What kind of girl do you think I am? You think you're so suave and charming. You feel threatened because Raimondo is so gallant. And what galls you even more, he's your ancestor. Well, you could learn a lot from him, Ray Almaviva. You may have his title, but you'll never have his class!" And she meant it to sting.

At that auspicious moment, Larry and Don Raimondo rolled in through the front door, as matey as a couple of sailors on shore leave.

"Did you get the *albariño?*" asked Ilsa sweetly.

"They didn't have that," said the Duke, "but we found a lovely *Godello*." He brandished four bottles. "And look," he said, holding up a newfound gadget. "They had this battery-operated corkscrew!" He pushed the button, and it whirled and whined. "What will they think of next?"

CHAPTER 30

THE AMERICA
THAT WE LOVE

In Ray's front room, standing around several card tables, Ray, Ilsa, Don Raimondo, and Larry were stamping out Almavivan passports like waffles. The line of applicants wound down the street and around the corner. Followed by her cameraman shouldering his camera, Monica Bingley was conducting interviews up and down the line. She held her microphone up to a middle-aged couple.

"Excuse me," asked Monica. "You're trading your US citizenship for an Almavivan passport?"

The cameraman zoomed in.

"You know what my paycheck's gonna look like without withholding income tax, social security tax, Medicare tax, Federal Unemployment tax, and local taxes?" said the man. "My wife has quit her job!"

The professional feminist in Monica was aghast. "You sacrificed your career?"

The wife primped for the camera. "Honey, you call bein' a secretary a career? I'm gonna take up pottery and...," snuggling her husband, "cuddle my love bug!" They squeezed with treacly affection.

Rolling her eyes, Monica scanned along the line until, to her amazement, she discovered the famous money guru, Charles Payne, in line. She shoved the mike in Payne's face and was gratified with a glossy smile and a sound bite: "It's the financially responsible thing to do!"

Moving along, Monica's astonishment grew as she spotted someone in dark sunglasses who appeared to be Greg Gutfeld. "Excuse me," she ventured.

"No! Hey! It's not me," exclaimed Gutfeld. "I'm just lucky enough to look like him."

Dubiously, Monica continued down the line. In a few moments, she recognized the unmistakable visage of Elon Musk! The inimitable entrepreneur looked squarely into Monica's camera and shrugged. "I couldn't wait until Trump's second term to say: 'IRS–you're fired!'"

Ray handed the passport stamp to Don Raimondo and took a break. He strolled down the block, shaking hands and accepting generous slaps on his back. A wave of enthusiasm rippled through the crowd. Spontaneously, someone shouted:

"Three cheers for the Duke of Almaviva!"

The throng erupted.

"Hip-hip-hooray!"

Ray was starting to feel rather grand about all this. Although Don Raimondo looked up from the passport desk and took a gracious bow, thinking the cheers were for him, it was Ray who burst into song.

SONG: *THE AMERICA THAT WE LOVE*

Ray: I don't care what you say,
It's a glorious day

Here in the Federal City.
Think of Lincoln up there
And of Farragut Square—
The monuments sure are pretty!

What would Washington say
If he could see us today
Looking down from above?
He'd say,
You can put it on track,
You can take it all back:
The America that we love!

A pizza delivery boy cycled along the sidewalk. He swerved, narrowly missing Ray, who nimbly skipped aside and sang the chorus.

Ray: There's no need for dismay
In the US of A,
The land of brotherly love.
Together we can achieve
Anything we believe
In the America that we love!

The crowd joined in the finale.

All: It's up to each one of us,
Unum e pluribus,
In the America that we love!
Oh, yeah,
The America that we love!

The crowd struck a picturesque tableau.

CHAPTER 31

DESPERATE TIMES

Across town, in the Oval Office, President Beau Haydn, Chief of Staff Nelson McGaffer, Press Secretary Daisy Katrina-Perdue, the Speaker of the House Fanny Villosi, House Minority Leader Kenny McMurphy, Majority Leader of the Senate Jack Boomer, Minority Leader of the Senate Fitch McCormack, and Chief Justice of the Supreme Court John Windsock were all assembled together. They were glued to Monica Bingley's live broadcast. Over the TV came the second and third cheers of the crowd outside Ray's apartment.

"Hip-hip-hooray! Hip-hip-hooray! Viva Almaviva!"

The President wheeled and snarled at McGaffer and Katrina-Perdue. "Do you see what you've done? You did all this. You see what you've done?" He could be nasty when riled.

"Sir," simpered McGaffer, pointing at Speaker Villosi, "it was a Congressional Committee that caused his arrest...."

Fanny bared a fang. "You rat!"

"It's true," snarled McGaffer.

"All right! Stop it!" cried Senator Boomer.

President Haydn sank onto the sofa, moaning softly. "My legacy...my legacy..."

McGaffer shot his cuffs, rallying in the crisis. "Sir, what we need is a fix." At this imbecilic statement of the obvious, Haydn lost control. He jumped up and hurled the nearest file at Don. The papers fluttered about the Oval Office, settling picturesquely like snowflakes.

"Of course, we need a fix!" yapped the President. "So fix it! Fix it!"

McGaffer stood with cool dignity as the papers floated down around him. "Mr. President," he said, brushing aside a falling page, "I propose we withdraw all Federal programs from this so-called Duchy of Almaviva."

Haydn narrowed his eyes. "What?"

"No Federal funding for schools, clinics, police, firefighters..."

Senator McCormack chimed in, relishing the thought. "Bring the place to a standstill!"

"And without matching Federal funds," cried Speaker Villosi with glee, "we can get the District of Columbia to hold back all local programs, too!"

"That's it," said McGaffer, coolly inspecting his manicure. "No social services whatsoever. They'll be marooned."

Haydn paced, like a caged lion, stroking his chin. Then he halted. "How will it poll?"

"How do you want it to poll?" asked McGaffer coolly.

"The public will see leadership, Mr. President," said Daisy. "A firm hand at the helm. Justice."

"Yeah," said Senator Boomer. "Why should these Almavivan

deadbeats get what others pay for?"

"Isn't that the point of entitlements?" asked Congressman McMurphy.

"Of course," said Speaker Villosi, "but only for people we like."

"People who vote for us," clarified Senator McCormack.

"Actually, I don't like most of the people who vote for us," said Senator Boomer.

"Who does?" asked Speaker Villosi.

"How about the people who don't vote for us?" asked Congressman McMurphy.

"Oh, I hate them," said Senator Boomer.

"Well," said Haydn, a smile spreading across his rubbery face like a wandering scar, "it's worth a try."

"And one other thing," said Fanny. "Nelson, check with the State Department and the CIA."

"Why?" asked McGaffer.

"Did their research determine whether this Duke of Almaviva has any living relatives? They might prove...useful."

"Wouldn't they have told us if they had?" asked Congressman McMurphy.

"They never tell us anything until it gets leaked to the press," said Senator Boomer sourly.

"Well, tell them this," hissed Speaker Villosi. "This rebel duke has snitched all the tax revenue covering their budgets. If they don't come up with the goods, they'll be spying with weather balloons, not satellites."

CHAPTER 32

THE FEDS
PULL THE PLUG

In Washington, D.C., the right things are endlessly debated and never done, but the wrong things are done almost as quickly as thought upon, to paraphrase Goethe. Very soon, the bad official news seeped into the neighborhood of Almaviva. The residents of the Duchy were on their own. All Federal funding of everything touching their lives had dried up.

Ray, Ilsa, Don Raimondo, and Larry stood in the middle of a town hall meeting of neighbors. Larry was reviewing, for the third time, the court documents sent over by the Feds. Then he set them down on Ray's coffee table and spoke to the nervous, murmuring flock. "OK, OK. Let's not panic."

"Not panic?" said one neighbor. "We got no more police!"

"No schools!" said his wife.

"No Medicare!" said a second neighbor.

"No Social Security!" said a third neighbor.

"No garbage removal," said the third neighbor's wife.

"We'll starve!" said the first neighbor.

"We'll be robbed!" cried the second.

"We'll die!" wailed his wife.

"We will not die!" shouted Ray. "Listen to this man. He's an attorney."

Phil DeLuca materialized from the shadows and cleared his throat. "You know," he said calmly, "you can buy all that stuff."

"What, are you crazy?" asked the first neighbor. "Buy police?"

"And schools?" asked his wife.

"And food stamps?" asked the second neighbor.

"What do you think the government does?" asked Phil. "They buy all that stuff."

"But they can afford it," protested the third neighbor's wife.

"Only with our money," said Ray, catching on.

"Exactly," said Phil. "And you can buy it better and cheaper."

"Better and cheaper than the U.S. Government?" asked the third neighbor.

"Without a doubt," smiled Phil.

"How?" asked the third neighbor's wife.

"Look," said Phil with infinite patience. "You're a housewife. When you buy something with your own money for your own use, you care about the price, and you care about the quality, right?"

"You bet," she said.

"OK," said Phil. "Suppose you buy something with your own money for someone else."

"Like a Christmas gift?" she asked.

"Exactly," said Phil. "Then you care what you pay, but you don't care about the quality."

"That's the kind of Christmas gift I get," said Larry.

"Now," said Phil, ignoring him, "suppose you buy something with someone else's money for someone else to use."

The light flipped on in Ray's bean. "I get it! Then you don't care what it costs, and you don't care how good it is!"

"Right," smiled Phil. "And that's the Federal Government! They're buying stuff for you with your money, so they don't care what it costs, and they don't care if it's any good."

"So we can buy better police?" asked the first neighbor.

"And firemen!" cried Ray enthusiastically. "And doctors!"

"And teachers!" declared Ilsa. "And insurance!"

"And everything!" boomed Larry.

"But where do we get the money?" asked the second neighbor.

"Don't you see?" said Ray. "We've already got the money! We've always had the money!"

Phil nodded. "You just don't let the Feds take it out in taxes, that's all! And not just payroll taxes, but property taxes, sales taxes, vehicle licensing taxes, business licensing taxes, telecommunication taxes, all of it! It adds up to a lot more than you think."

The whole crowd of neighbors was awestruck. They were a dozen minds with a single thought. In hushed tones, the first neighbor spoke for them all: "Freedom!"

CHAPTER 33

PARIS ON
THE POTOMAC

The presidential helicopter hovered daintily before coming to rest on the White House lawn. The rush from its rotors tested the staying power of hair gel among the huddling Press Corps. As the chopper settled on the grass and the whine of the rotors lowered in pitch, the gangway dropped, and President Haydn emerged. Unfortunately, he tripped while exiting. McGaffer, his Chief of Staff, hastened to help him back to his feet. The President dusted bits of turf off his trousers. Then he smartly saluted the Marine Guard, but unfortunately, he was facing the wrong way. The Marine Guard remained frozen in a stiff salute to his Commander-in-Chief. McGaffer turned the President around. When he was finally facing the Marine Guard, Haydn said, "Didn't I salute you already? Oh, well," and he saluted again.

With a smug expression behind his dark aviator glasses, which he hoped would make even an octogenarian seem cool, Haydn attempted to put on his jacket, but could not find one of the sleeves. Reaching for the sleeve hole, he made several full rotations until one of his aids stepped in, held his coat for him, and put him out of his misery. Resuming a look of confidence, the President sauntered across the lawn, waving at the Press, pretending, almost convincingly, that he was unaware of the hoarse chorus of frantic questions. He wandered off course into the bushes, but McGaffer steered him back on track, and the Leader of the Free World vanished through the White House doors.

Inside the Oval Office, his Press Secretary, Daisy Katrina-Purdue, surged to the President's side. "Sir," she ventured in a strangled whisper, "there's an update on TV."

Haydn's optimism rose to the surface. "Ready to surrender, are they?"

Daisy looked down at the ground. "Um..." She snapped on the big, flat-screen TV. There was no need to browse channels. Every station was carrying it. But this happened to be WONK-TV, and Monica Bingley was doing a stand-up piece on the camera.

"More astonishing developments in the case that is being called Duke-gate," she said, in the singsong, self-important tone that TV newsreaders spend hours in the bathroom perfecting. Panning the boulevards of Almaviva, the camera drank in an entirely new appearance of this once slightly shabby neighborhood of the Federal City. The streets had sprouted with outdoor cafés, festooned with colorful parasols. Tables were crowded with languid citizens sporting striped t-shirts, berets, and floral skirts.

"Despite the withdrawal of police protection and all Federal programs from this small, Washington neighborhood," intoned Monica, "the Duchy of Almaviva becoming rather like Paris on the Potomac."

Monica turned to an ex-plumber, who was sipping a chalice of ruby-colored Lussac-Sainte-Émilion in a sidewalk bistro. "You, sir...," she began, as the camera zoomed on his urbane, mildly bored expression.

"Ye-as?" enquired the ex-plumber.

"You used to be a plumber here?"

"Too true."

"And now?"

"Well, I was a little miffed when the Feds scrambled our satellite TV. But, with all the dough I'm saving on tax money, I took French lessons, and now I find reading Dumas in the original is much more absorbing than *Wheel of Fortune*...."

Monica boggled.

In the Oval Office, the presidential jaw hung slack. His staff exchanged pained glances.

On camera, Monica moved along, putting the mic to three teenagers, who formed an accordion, violin, and bass trio on the sidewalk. They were, in fact, the same hoodlums who had once bashed into the apparel shop on the day of the Capitol protest. They played a lively version of the Charles Trenet song, *Ménilmontant*, filling the neighborhood with a romantic air.

"Excuse me," ventured Monica, approaching the girl playing the violin in the trio.

"Yes?" said the girl, playing exquisitely without pause.

"How are you kids doing since the lack of Federal funds closed down your school?"

"Oh, at first, we were kinda bummed," she said, still playing.

"But," added another kid, playing the bass with verve, "our moms and dads pooled the tax money they saved and got us tutors."

"Yeah," said the accordionist, "and the tutors got us through the whole eighth grade in three months...."

"And with the extra time and money..." said the violinist, still playing suavely.

"We started our own trio," said the bass player.

"Not bad, huh?" asked the accordionist.

Monica looked into the camera, raising a frankly astonished eyebrow. "Well, there you have it," she told her viewers. Then her glance alighted on two young men ambling up the sidewalk. They were dressed like Italian *carabinieri* in tall, plumed hats, golden epaulets, crimson sashes, and silver braids. They saluted politely as they passed. Monica nodded to her cameraman and pursued them.

"Excuse me, officers...."

"Ma'am?" asked the first officer.

"We understood that since Almavivans were in tax revolt—all police protection had been withdrawn."

"That's true, ma'am," confirmed the second officer.

"But we took up a collection from everyone in the neighborhood," said the first officer.

"And we started our own police force," smiled the second officer.

"Is it working?" asked Monica.

The two officers exchanged grins.

"Check the statistics, ma'am," said the first officer.

"We've gone from one of the highest crime neighborhoods in America...," said the second officer.

"To the lowest," said the first.

Monica swallowed before asking the next delicate question.

"Is it true that you officers all used to be...uh, gang bangers?"

The officers winced. But their nobler nature prevailed. "We don't like to dwell on our unsavory past," said the second officer.

"But, yes, that is the case," confessed the first officer.

"That's one reason the crime rate has gone down so drastically," grinned the second officer.

"Yeah," cackled the first officer. *"We're* off the streets!"

Reverting to old habits, the two *carabinieri* doubled up and gave each other a fist bump. But, quickly recovering their new-found dignity, they stiffened, straightened their plumed helmets, saluted Monica, and resumed their stately patrol.

The street in front of Ray's apartment had been closed off to traffic, becoming a promenade where the Almavivans enjoyed the open-air delights of an early Spring in their beautiful Duchy. Ray and Ilsa walked down the street, but still estranged, on opposite sides. Don Raimondo followed along with Ilsa, while Larry walked with Ray. The French café music of the trio swept them along. Now celebrities of a sort among the Almavivans, Ray and Ilsa greeted friends and neighbors on every side as they strolled along. Inspired by the festive atmosphere, Ray burst into song.

SONG: *PARIS ON THE POTOMAC*

Ray: You can travel the earth,
But right here you will find
Paris on the Potomac!

Not to be outdone, Ilsa picked up the song's next line, interrupting Ray, who furrowed his brow.

Ilsa: No treasure is worth
The attainments refined
Of Paris on the Potomac.

Taking back control of the song, Ray continued:

Ray: Each citizen here can read music and paint,
And our statues have run out of pigeons!

Taking it away, Ilsa resumed:

Ilsa: We're all multilingual and cultured and quaint,
In own little slice of Paree,

And taking it back, Ray concluded:

Ray: *Mai oui,*

Both, in harmony: In our own little slice of Paree.

A taxi driver leaned out of his car window and sang the next verse.

Taxi Driver: We used to be boorish
And sloppy and crass,
Relying on Federal assistance.

A lady shopper, laden with shiny shopping bags, picked up the song in a Southern accent.

Lady Shopper: Now see how we flourish
With style and class–
What a beautiful form of existence!

A waiter in one of the cafés, dressed in a crimson vest and jet-black bow tie, joined in.

Waiter: We shudder to think of how once we relied
On uncouth entitlement handouts!

A lady café patron, sitting at a table, being served by the waiter, and holding a miniature poodle in her lap, joined in.

Lady: We're better off now, and we take rightful pride.
In our own little slice of Paree,

Everyone on the street sang in chorus.

All: *Mai ouí,*
In our own little slice of Paree.

The accordionist played a virtuoso cadenza as the people got up
and danced up and down the promenade. The waiter pirouetted
over to Ray and Ilsa and handed each of them a flute of champagne.
Ray gazed at Ilsa, who gazed back. There remained a touch of frost
between them. But the music was soft, inviting. They melted a
bit and clicked their glasses together and took a sip. Ray reached
for Ilsa's hand, but she demurely set her flute down and strolled
away from him. Ray set his flute down and followed her. Everyone
smiled at him and patted his back as he walked among them, but he
only had eyes for Ilsa. The crowd grew considerably, and at the end
of the accordion cadenza, everyone in the street joined in a robust,
final verse.

All: We will never go back
To the way that we were,
A slum in the Federal city.
We're on the right track,

All; [Spoken] *Élégance de rigueur!*

All: Discerning, insightful, and witty.
We rose up ourselves and became what we are
Without bureaucratic assistance!
We're on our life's journey, pursuing our star,
In our own little slice of Paree,

Mai ouí,
In our own little slice of Paree.

The trio continued to play the enchanting melody. Ray again offered Ila his left hand. She hesitated, but then modestly surrendered it to him. Ray put his right hand on Ilsa's waist. She smiled. They began waltzing around the promenade to the tune. All the people on the promenade were now paired off and waltzing, creating a dazzling scene of festivity and color. As the instrumental trio neared the end of the tune, Ray sang to Ilsa with feeling, "We're on our life's journey, pursuing our star."

Ilsa sang back: "In our own little slice of Paree."

Ray: *Ma chérie!*

Both: "In our own little slice of Paree!"

The music stopped. Ilsa lingered in Ray's embrace. A little embarrassed and a little confused, they stepped apart from each other.

Monica, resuming her report, turned and addressed her camera. "What was intended as punitive action by the Federal government," she chanted, "turning into unexpected relief for the Duchy. With Federal education funds gone, test scores for Almavivan kids are soaring! With Medicare gone, the people of Almaviva have enough disposable income from tax savings to put up their own private hospitals. They've gone from being among the poorest to some of the wealthiest folks in America. The Almavivan Miracle left leading politicians baffled, saying...."

Back in the Oval Office, President Haydn grabbed the TV remote and hurled it at the screen shouting, "Damn! Damn! Damn!

Damn! Damn!"

"Sir...," ventured McGaffer.

"This has got to be illegal!" ranted the President. "Get the Attorney General! I want this in front of the Supreme Court tomorrow!"

"Sir," said the Chief of Staff, "the Supreme Court has already ruled. However, the CIA has come up with something."

CHAPTER 34

EVICTED

Ray, Ilsa, Don Raimondo, Larry, and Phil were sipping red wine in Ray's apartment. Phil savored it approvingly. "Excellent," he said.

"Like it?" asked Don Raimondo. "We call it Almavivan Red."

"It's bottled in California," explained Ray, "but the winery wanted to use our name. Oh, and they are now headquartered here, too."

Phil smiled knowingly. "Every Duchy should have its own vintage," he said.

"That's what I thought," said Ilsa.

Larry tapped the pleadings stacked on the coffee table. "Is this really possible...?"

"It's perfectly legal," said Phil.

"Isn't it a bit over the top?" asked Ray.

"It's a pre-emptive strike," said Phil, swirling the wine in his glass meditatively. "I'm sure the other side is planning one."

"So we don't really have a choice?" asked Ray.

"That's my view," said Phil.

"Ray," gulped Larry, "are we really gonna...?"

Ray took an appreciative sip of Almavivan Red. "What do you think, Ilsa?"

"You're asking me? Oh, well, in that case: file the papers, Larry. File the papers."

Hardly surprising, thought Ray. Given a choice, Ilsa would always walk on the edge.

To Larry, the room seemed to reel around. "Omigosh!" he blurted. "It's a lawyer's fantasy!"

Phil's features split in a rare smile so wide it almost met in the back. Ray patted Larry on the shoulder.

The next day, at the Supreme Court Building, a slightly inebriated process server and two cops stopped Chief Justice John Windsock and the eight other Justices as they swept in imperial majesty through their private entrance. "Mr. Chief Justice?" slurred the process server.

"Ye-as," said the Man in Black pompously.

The process server swallowed, but the saliva wouldn't come. He had fortified himself with two quick snootfuls before undertaking this tremendous task, but at the critical moment, his fluid fortitude deserted him.

"You'll have to evacuate these premises, sir."

The Chief Justice staggered. "I beg your pardon..."

The process server squirmed. "Please read the order, sir. It's all valid."

The Chief Justice exchanged incredulous glances with his eight learned colleagues. He took the papers impatiently and read: "Know all men by these presents...blah, blah, blah...whereas His Grace, the Duke of the Duchy of Almaviva...blah, blah, blah...."

Another Justice peered over his shoulder and continued reading: "The Supreme Court building is...?"

A third Justice, crowding in, took over: "...illegitimately occupies the sovereign territory of the Duchy of Almaviva...!"

A fourth Justice glared at the document. "You've got to be kidding..."

A fifth, rather elderly Justice, stared blankly. "I don't understand..."

"Another fine mess you've got us into," said the sixth Justice to the Chief Justice.

In mere moments, nine Justices in black, flowing robes were tottering out of the Supreme Court building, evacuating. Monica Bingley and her cameraman were on hand, with hordes of other media, on a tip from the increasingly efficient Almavivan Press Office (Ilsa).

Monica brushed a strand of hair out of her eyes and hastily began an on-camera stand-up report. "Not since the War of 1812 has a foreign power evicted a branch of the U.S. Government from Washington, D.C." With impeccable timing, she thrust her microphone at the Chief Justice as he passed. "Mr. Chief Justice, is it true that the Court is being charged with rent unpaid to the Duke of Almaviva since the building was put up in 1935?"

"Oh, shut up!" came the learned reply.

CHAPTER 35

THE IMPOSTER

Soon afterward, the nine Supremes, homeless now, moped about the Oval Office with the President, McGaffer, and Katrina-Purdue. They peered at a wall map showing the shape of the Duchy of Almaviva superimposed on Washington, D.C. The Chief Justice pointed to the blob of the Duchy that enveloped the Supreme Court.

"It's just bad luck," he said in a strangled sob, "that the Duchy sits here where the Supreme Court used to be."

"Pull yourself together!" snarled McGaffer.

Squinting at the map, Daisy remarked: "It won't end there."

"What do you mean?" asked the President.

"The Duchy covers the whole of D.C., including Capitol Hill and...."

"Not the White House!" gurgled the President.

"I'm afraid so," said Daisy.

"Are you telling me they're going to try to evict us even from here?"

The phone hummed. McGaffer picked it up. "Yes?" He covered the receiver. "Mr. President, Secretary Cleaver, and the parties you wanted to see...."

"Who?" asked Haydn.

"The Secretary of State and those foreign dignitaries the CIA dug up," said McGaffer.

"Ah, yes!" said Haydn, rubbing his hands. "Show them in!"

The door to the Oval Office opened by the unseen hand of a Marine Guard. Secretary of State Wilson Cleaver admitted a flamboyantly dressed Spaniard, who, on close inspection, proved to be the spitting image of Ray Almaviva. In with him swanked Luisa Cabana, a shady lady from Argentina, who recalled Carmen Miranda, less the fruity hat. Both spoke with exaggerated Spanish accents. Before anyone could stop him, Don Ricardo and Luisa broke into an Andalusian song.

SONG: *WITH DUCAL HAUTEUR AND BEARING*

Don Ricardo: With ducal hauteur and bearing
And all my medallions wearing
I come here to claim
My legal domain
With all of my rights declaring.

Don Ricardo danced a dramatic flamenco for a few bars, finishing the last measure by striking a pose. Luisa carried on with the following verse.

Luisa: The nobility in his glances
And the dignified way he dances

Clearly reveal
He's the genuine deal,
Under the circumstances.

Don Ricardo and Luisa then danced the flamenco with considerable verve. When done, they resumed singing together.

Both: Enough of this usurpation!
Get on with our coronation!
Throw that fraudster in jail
Without any bail
Or wearisome litigation!

The President and his entourage watched, speechless, as Don Ricardo and Luisa got another few bars of flamenco dancing out of their system. They concluded by singing the finale ensemble.

Both: So, lock up that fraud
And let us applaud
Our legitimate installation!

The pair came to a stately finish. Then Don Ricardo gushed. "Mr. President! May I present my fiancée, Luisa Cabana?"

The President regarded her as if he were a Czar inspecting a kulak.

"Meester President," oozed Luisa, "You are such an inspiration to the weemens of the world!"

"I am?" mumbled the President. Turning to Daisy, he asked, "I am?"

McGaffer took over. "Have a seat, Don Ricardo. Shall we get down to brass tacks?"

"Sure, sure!" grinned Don Ricardo. "Let's get down to the brash tactics."

McGaffer turned to Secretary Cleaver. "Now, as I understand it, Don Ricardo here may hold a legitimate claim to the title of the American Duke...?"

"May?" blurted Luisa, astonished. "May? Oh, no, Mr. President. I assure you, he is the legitimate *duca*."

Don Ricardo drew himself up. "I am the direct descendant of Don Raimondo de Borbón y Cortés, Count of Almaviva!"

Luisa slapped the President heartily on the back. "You can take it to the bank!" She emitted a shattering laugh.

McGaffer turned to Cleaver. "The CIA affirms it?"

Cleaver shuffled. "Well, it's a difficult problem."

"Difficult?" snorted Luisa. "Oh, no, but you are mistaken. This other one, he is imposter!"

Cleaver patiently unrolled a massive family tree and laid it across the President's desk.

"Well, um, the thing is, sir, the original Count Almaviva, as he once was, having been created Duke of Almaviva, as he then became, by Act of the Continental Congress, of course, returned to Europe after the Revolution with his cousin, the Marquis de Lafayette, to carry on the revolutionary struggle against the French King, Louis XVI. Always the adventurer, he marched with the emperor Napoleon, as he then was, across Europe, where he, Don Raimondo, not Napoleon, I mean, died at the Battle of Austerlitz in an unfortunate encounter with a cannon."

"Really?" asked Don Ricardo in amazement.

McGaffer was annoyed. "Look, is this man heir to the title or not?"

"Of course he is!" gushed Luisa. "He has nobility written on his chicks!"

"Chicks?" asked Haydn, uncomprehending.

Luisa pinched Don Ricardo's cheeks. "Sure! Chicks!"

The President's brow furrowed.

"I'm sorry, Mr. President," said Cleaver woefully. "It is a little complex..."

"Pray continue," said McGaffer.

Cleaver cleared his throat. "You see," he said, "Don Raimondo had two sons, twins. One stayed in Europe and was the twenty-fourth ancestor of Don Ricardo. The other returned to Virginia in 1816 and was the twenty-fourth ancestor of Ray Almaviva."

Daisy pointed at Don Ricardo as if he were an object in a museum. "So this man could be the rightful Duke?"

"Is, *Señora!*" said Don Ricardo, indignantly.

"But you see the problem, sir," interjected Cleaver. "Twins. And no record of which was born first."

"No clear right of primogeniture," opined Chief Justice Windsock, pedantically.

There was a moment of silence. Then McGaffer said, "It's good enough for me!" Looking sternly at Don Ricardo, he challenged: "Are you prepared to fight for your birthright?"

"To the death!" gushed Luisa.

"To the death?" asked Don Ricardo, aghast.

Taking Luisa aside, he whispered, "*Querida*, there is no point fighting for my birthright to the death! What good is dying for what I was born to enjoy?"

"Well," said Luisa to the assembly, "to exhaustion then. He will fight to exhaustion!"

"Yes, Meester President," declared Don Ricardo with pride. "I would fight until I was very, very tired."

McGaffer rolled his eyes. "Well, I'm very, very tired of this mess. I want the Supreme Court," he jabbed a finger at the Justices, "to write a legal opinion that Don Ricardo is the rightful Duke."

"That's the ticket," said the President.

The Nine Justices bristled. The Chief Justice cleared his throat. "Mr. President, we can't just write an opinion like that."

"It takes research, weighty consideration, the fullness of time," added another Justice.

"And our clerks," added another Justice. "They do all the work."

"Do you want the Supreme Court Building back?" growled McGaffer. "Because it's fine with me! We can just set you up in the break room at the Bureau of Indian Affairs!"

"I must protest," cried another Justice.

"All you have to do," said McGaffer, "is render a unanimous opinion."

Another Justice shrugged. "It *is* only a question of genealogy. It's not as though we have to do the impossible, like define what a woman is."

"I suppose," mused the Chief Justice.

"It's settled then," said McGaffer. Businesslike, he turned to Don Ricardo. "Now you—you will sign over the Duchy of Almaviva to the United States...."

"But not, I hope," interjected Luisa, "without equitable...," groping for the word, "compensation...."

"I think that is understood," said Don Ricardo genially.

President Haydn adopted a formal tone. "I will ask Congress to appropriate $50,000 per year from the Duchy's creation until this date."

"Ah, but *Señor*," demurred Luisa, "that is only...." She made a lightning calculation. "Eleven-point-three million dollars."

"Only?" asked McGaffer acidly.

Don Ricardo gently cleared his throat. "Oddly enough, Meester President, before coming here, I had a very e-stimulating interview with the ambassador of China."

"That snake!" snarled McGaffer.

"Yes," said Don Ricardo urbanely. "That *e-snake*. And it seems that Beijing, if given the chance to buy my Duchy, well...they would value it...rather more highly."

"Much more highly," said Luisa.

McGaffer turned purple, attempting to strangle his fury. "How much?"

"One hundred billion," purred Luisa.

"One hundred billion!" spluttered McGaffer.

"Dollars," clarified Luisa.

"In a Cayman Islands account," added Don Ricardo. "If we have learned anything from this Duchy of Almaviva business, *Señor*, it is that one must be mindful of taxes...."

Stifling rage, McGaffer turned tight-lipped to Daisy. "The first Duke of Almaviva swiped the Spanish Treasure Fleet?"

"Well...yes," answered Daisy.

McGaffer trained narrowed eyes on Don Ricardo and remarked: "So this pirate really could be the Duke...."

CHAPTER 36

HARDBALL

In the Oval Office, at night, McGaffer, in rolled-up shirt sleeves, reviewed plan details with President Haydn and Major General Earl Undershot, Chief of the Joint Chiefs of Staff.

"It's all set?" asked McGaffer.

"Yes, sir," rumbled General Undershot. "The entire perimeter will be sealed at dawn. Sir?"

"Yes?" asked McGaffer.

"I was speaking to the President," said the General, stuffily.

The President, however, was napping peacefully at the Resolute desk.

"Yes?" repeated McGaffer, pointedly.

"Well, we could take out their HQ with a single drone," said the General. He made a gesture and a whining sound like a dive bomber, followed by an exploding sound, "Bam!" McGaffer was dumbfounded. He glared, wondering how some people get to be generals. Then he remembered. They didn't earn it. Captains earned it. Majors earned it. Colonels earned it. They rose through the ranks. But generals are appointed by the President. He glanced at the slumbering Commander in Chief, and all became clear. Then he said loftily: "No shooting without the President's orders, General."

"Yes, sir," said General Undershot. "How will we know when he gives them?" he asked, arching an eyebrow at the snoozing President.

"I'll let you know," said McGaffer.

At the same time, not far away, Ilsa was making her way toward the Duchy of Almaviva. But the streets of Washington, D.C. had assumed the appearance of a war zone. Military patrols were whizzing about. Army engineers were unraveling huge, razor wire coils around the Almavivan frontier and were erecting guard shacks at fortified checkpoints. Searchlights swept the streets. Ilsa approached a checkpoint with a sense of dread.

"Your papers," demanded the Marine Guard on duty.

Ilsa fumbled for her driver's license. The Marine Guard took it. "Just a moment, ma'am."

He swiped her license into a computer at the guard shack. The screen flashed: ACCESS DENIED. The Marine Guard drilled Ilsa with a steely gaze. "Ma'am, you'll have to come along with me for questioning."

"What?" blurted Ilsa. "Why?"

"I'm sorry, ma'am, that will be addressed in questioning."

The Marine gestured to a pair of MPs, who moved toward Ilsa. An inexplicable thrill shot up her spine. "Run!" she shouted to herself. She took her own advice and bolted. She pelted through the checkpoint into Almavivan Territory. The MPs smartly took aim with their rifles, but the Marine Lieutenant checked them. "Hold your fire. Put out a bulletin. Hook her up the next time she tries to come through."

"Yes, sir," said an MP, with an air of disappointment.

Across the frontier, an eerie quiet prevailed. Ilsa found the street outside Ray's apartment dappled in moonbeams, and she leaped from shadow to shadow toward his house. Inside, Ray, Don Raimondo, Larry, and Phil were standing around the kitchen table, looking haggard. But Ray brightened at the sight of Ilsa.

"Do you know what's happening?" she asked breathlessly.

Phil held up a document between two nicely manicured fingers. "We read all about it."

Ray pursed his lips. "Unless we surrender by—" he consulted his watch—"five a.m., they're going to—"

The lights went out.

"Cut out the lights," finished Larry.

"It's five a.m.," said Ilsa.

Taking a hurricane lamp off a shelf, Don Raimondo struck a match and lit it. The yellow glow bathed the room, blending gradually over the next few minutes with the coming dawn. The door creaked, and one by one, Ray's crestfallen neighbors began oozing into the apartment, their faces etched with anxiety.

"What happened?" asked the first neighbor.

"Did you see what's out there?" asked the second. "Marines!"

"Barbed wire fences!" quivered the third.

"We're in a concentration camp!" wailed the first neighbor's wife.

"We're going to die!" prophesied the second neighbor's wife apocalyptically.

"We're not going to die," said Ray decisively.

Phil DeLuca slowly rose. "I don't know about dying, Ray, but this is where CE packs it in."

"You're abandoning us?" choked Larry.

"It's what we call *force majeure*, son. So long, Your Grace. And good luck."

The neighbors watched gloomily as the lawyer in the ostentatiously expensive suit sauntered out.

"There goes one of the biggest corporations in the world," groaned the third neighbor.

"It's over," said the first neighbor. "And look," he cried, holding up his smartphone. "They've scrambled our cell phones! No internet!"

"We're condemned," moaned the second neighbor.

"We're not condemned," insisted Ray.

At that moment, a Marine Lieutenant at the checkpoint blared over a loudspeaker. "Citizens of Almaviva: your neighborhood is condemned."

The neighbors all turned on Ray. "See?" they chorused.

"Due to non-payment of your taxes," continued the Lieutenant, "and unlawful insurrection against the United States of America, your water, power, and freedom have been cut off. You have seven hours to surrender peacefully. All who do so by high noon will be treated fairly. All who resist will be placed under arrest and will be treated as prisoners of war."

"Guantanamo!" cried the first neighbor. "We're going to Guantanamo!"

"Can they do that?" asked the second neighbor.

The third neighbor shifted from foot to foot. "I've known you a long time, Ray, but...."

"What's the use?" whimpered the first neighbor's wife.

"I'm outta here," concluded the third neighbor.

"Me, too," agreed his wife.

"Good luck, buddy," said the second neighbor.

And, with a wistful backward glance, the entire committee of neighbors shuffled out into the new dawn. Their voices echoed from outside as they called to the MPs:

"Don't shoot!"

"We surrender!"

"We're unarmed!"

"Now what, Ray?" asked Larry.

Ray paced up and down, rubbing the stubble on his chin. Then he sighed. "Ilsa, Larry, Don Raimondo,...why don't you all go, too?"

Don Raimondo was indignant. "An Almaviva? Surrender? Never!"

Ilsa shook her head. "I'm not leaving you, Ray."

"I'd like to stay, too," said Larry.

Ray was moved by the show of loyalty from this remnant of his family and friends. But, no, this was unfair. "It's me they're after," he said.

"No," said Ilsa, "it's all of us they're after. You're just in their way."

"Well, maybe. I guess you really can't fight City Hall after all. Look, now I am City Hall, in a funny, old way. And it's harder being City Hall than it looks."

"At least you stand for something," said Ilsa, proudly.

Ray felt the kindling of an inner fire. "You know what I should have stood for? All these years? It sounds corny but for God, family, and country. It's just like Edmund Burke said..." Ray paused. "What did he say?" he asked Ilsa.

All it takes for evil to prevail is for good men to do nothing," she said, obligingly.

"And my whole life, I did nothing," said Ray. "Don Raimondo!"

"Yes," said the ancestor.

"You are the perfect example of a good man doing something. You captured the Treasure Fleet, you supplied the Revolution, and because of you, the world changed."

"But not for the better, as far as I can see," said Don Raimondo. "The country I helped to found has become an ugly tyranny, founded by geniuses but run by idiots. I wish I had never given Washington that gold."

"What gold?" asked Larry.

"That's not the point," said Ray, ignoring Larry. "The point is you did what you could. You made a difference. What other people do, how the world reacts, you can't help that. But you did all you could. And so will I."

At that moment, the roar of many voices erupted outside. With a bang, the door of Ray's apartment blew open, and the committee of neighbors swept back in. Now their faces were flushed with hope.

"Ray!" exclaimed the first neighbor. "You're not gonna believe this!" Gesturing wildly for Ray to follow him outside, the second neighbor shouted, "Come on!"

Part Four

In politics, strangely enough, the
best way to play your cards is to lay them
face upwards on the table.

—H.G. Wells

CHAPTER 37

AIRLIFT

On the other side of the Almavivan frontier, throngs of American citizens had gathered, chanting and carrying signs. News helicopters hovered overhead. The Marines were uncomfortably sandwiched between an angry mob and the security wall that penned the Almavivans in.

"Protestors!" shouted Ilsa.

"Look at the signs," grinned Don Raimondo.

The multitude was carrying placards that read: VIVA ALMAVIVA! WE LOVE THE DUKE! SHRED THE FEDS! In the distance, the sound of a people's chorus empurpled the air with song.

SONG: *THE RIGHTS OF MAN*

All: Hurrah for the Rights of Man!
Equality is nature's plan!
We're created to be free,

And we'll never bend a knee,
But fight for that great birthright,
Our noble, global birthright,
Our birthright since the world began!

"They're on our side," laughed Larry.

"Everybody's gone crazy!" gushed Ilsa. She gripped Ray's arm. Ray touched her hands. They both felt a little *frisson* of, of...but there was no time for that now. The protestors defiantly jabbed flowers down the rifle barrels of the Marines, chanting: "Hey, hey! Ho, ho! Let the Almavivans go!" Then the crowd began to pitch cans of cola and chocolate bars over the barbed wire. Ray's neighbors ran gratefully to pick them up. Ray, Ilsa, and Larry exchanged grins.

"Airlift!" cried Larry. "It's an airlift!"

The Marines rustled up a phalanx to try blocking the rations being chucked over the barbed wire, but they were soon overwhelmed by the throng, who pitched a hailstorm of water bottles, soda cans, and snacks over their heads. A can of garbanzo beans bonked the helmet of one hapless Marine, causing him to stumble. The mob roared in defiance. In disgust, the Marine dropped his rifle, grabbed a sign, and joined the protesters.

In a news helicopter wobbling overhead, Monica Bingley broadcast the bird's eye view in the TV newscaster's regulation sentence fragments: "Unbelievable. At least two thousand people turning out to support the Almavivans behind the blockade. This reporter hasn't seen anything like it since the Capitol riot! The American people showing once again how much we love the underdog!"

In the midst of the glorious turmoil, Ray pulled Ilsa, Larry, and Don Raimondo into a huddle. "I've got a plan," he said. "Ilsa, think you could squeak back through that checkpoint?" He pointed.

Ilsa squinted at the Marines struggling with the throbbing crowd. "Well... OK, sure!"

"They'll shoot you!" said Larry.

"They won't shoot her," said Ray. "Me, they might."

"They gotta catch me first!" Ilsa grinned.

"All you've got to do," said Ray, "is get to an unblocked cell phone."

"And then?" asked Ilsa.

"And then...I want you to make a few simple calls..."

CHAPTER 38

NEVER FEAR!
WE ARE HERE!

Inside the Oval Office, the President and his team, including Don Ricardo and Luisa, were huddled around the big, flat-screen monitor, watching WONK-TV with Monica Bingley on camera. Behind her were the swelling crowds at the Almavivan frontier, now in the tens of thousands.

"We're receiving reports," said Monica, "that five million Americans are planning to march on the capital, and look at this...."

The camera cut to a convoy of trucks, with American flags streaming, barreling east with crowds cheering them on both sides of the highway as far back as the eye could see.

"Convoys of freedom-loving truckers heading to the nation's capital. I don't know if you can hear me," shouted Monica to her network anchor, "but the folks are chanting, 'Mr. President, tear down this wall!'"

In the Oval Office, Haydn wheeled savagely on McGaffer. "I'm being cast as Gorbachev here!" he yelped.

"Surely not, Mr. President," said Daisy. "No one will think that."

Luisa, gawking at the chaos on TV, mused, "No. They will theenk Heetler."

The President erupted. "Dammit, McGaffer, I'm about to be the first president since James Buchanan to have part of the country secede from the Union! What could be worse?" His voice rose an octave, wavered, and broke. "What the hell could possibly be worse?"

As if in answer to the President's metaphysical query, a United Nations limo with tinted windows purred up to the Almavivan checkpoint. The chauffeur rolled down the window and told the Marine Lieutenant, in a bored, third-party sort of way, "The General Secretary of the United Nations requests a diplomatic pass to cross the Almavivan frontier."

From inside the perimeter fence, Ray, Larry, and Don Raimondo pushed to the front of the crowd of neighbors and peered at the long, black car flying the twin blue flags. The rear passenger door cracked open, and Ilsa bobbed out, waving and grinning. "Hey! Hey!" she called.

"She did it!" said Larry.

The Marines glared at each other under furrowed brows. The neighbors exploded in a Rebel yell. "Yee-hah!"

The Marine Lieutenant got in radio contact with General Undershot, requesting orders. "Sir, this is Checkpoint Charlie."

"Eagle One," said General Undershot. "Come in, Checkpoint Charlie."

"Sir, what do I do about this limousine?"

"What limousine?" enquired Undershot.

"The one filled with United Nations ambassadors, sir."

The General gave a quizzical look at McGaffer. "You can't pick a fight with the whole United Nations," said the Chief of Staff. "Let them pass."

"Let them pass, Lieutenant," ordered the General.

And the limousine slid through Checkpoint Charlie.

"Over here!" cried Ray, waving.

Shortly after, Ray and his entourage received their distinguished guests in Ray's living room. Ilsa opened the door and, with all the pomp of a Buckingham Palace footman, formally announced: "Her Excellency, the Secretary General of the United Nations, Dr. Mimsy Borogrove."

An elegant Ugandan glided into the room, wearing colorful, traditional African robes. She bowed with poise. "Your Grace."

Ray returned the bow as if to the manor born. "Madame Secretary."

"His Excellency," announced Ilsa, "the French ambassador, Monsieur Emile Débris!"

Bowing unctuously, the Frenchman effused: *"Monsieur le duc! Enchanté."*

"His Excellency," said Ilsa, "the German ambassador, Herr Otto Zeufer."

A stocky Prussian with steel-grey eyes clicked his heels smartly. *"Mein Lieber Herzog!"*

"How do you do?" replied Ray. "My cousin, Raimondo," he added.

Otto glared speculatively at Don Raimondo through his monocle. Don Raimondo glared back.

"Her Excellency, the Chinese ambassador, Heidi Ho," said Ilsa.

Ray and Madame Ho exchanged bows.

"Her Excellency, Heather McFly, ambassador from the United Kingdom," said Ilsa.

"My pleasure," said Heather, extending her hand. Ray shook it cordially.

"And His Excellency, the Russian ambassador, Aleksandr Myrmidon." Ray and the Russian ambassador bowed to each other.

Mimsy Borogrove introduced the business motif.

"Your Grace, we are intrigued by your proposal."

"And?" asked Ray.

"We would, of course, like to invite the Duchy into the United Nations."

"Fine!" beamed Ray.

"But we cannot," said Otto.

"Why?" asked Larry.

"The American veto, *naturellement*," said Emile, with distaste.

"Then what about my second proposal?" asked Ray.

Mimsy weighed her words carefully. "Your Grace...the United Nations, and especially Germany and France, are prepared to express solidarity with the Duchy of Almaviva...."

"The rest of the world, *monsieur le duc*, is too tired of America throwing her weight around," said Emile.

"It's time for the lone superpower to start showing some respect," growled Otto.

The diplomats expressed their sentiments by breaking into song.

SONG: *NEVER FEAR! WE ARE HERE!*

Mimsy: Never Fear! We are here!
We have come to lend an ear.

Emile: Join the fellowship of nations,
And your troubles disappear!

Heather: In a jam with Uncle Sam?
Well, we got your telegram!

Otto: All of us United Nations
Are behind your aspirations!

Heidi: We can push, we can nudge,
And as history's our judge,

Aleksandr: The Americans will always buckle under!

All Six: Come on, unfurl your flag,
Don't be a punching bag!
Never fear!
Get in gear!
We are here!

Emile, Otto, and Aleksandr: Time to roar, this is war,
We will be your guarantor.
We'll make speeches on the beaches,
We're the diplomatic corps!

Mimsy, Heidi, and Heather: You're alone and afraid?
Feeling cheated and betrayed?

Emile, Otto, and Aleksandr: Well, my friend, don't feel
dejected!
You're so very well-connected!

Mimsy, Heidi, and Heather: We have tricks up our sleeve
That will bring you a reprieve,

Emile, Otto, and Aleksandr: And the whole world will
applaud for you like thunder!

All Six: Come on, unsheathe your sword,
And claim your just reward!
Never fear!
Dry that tear!
We are here!

The six ambassadors linked arms for a high-kicking chorus line
finish.

All Six: Don't let the District of Columbia
Overwhelm or overcome ya!
Never fear!
Just like Paul Revere,
We are here!

"So, you're on my side?" asked Ray, recovering from the
unexpected burst of song.

The three ambassadors shifted uncomfortably.

"We're not on their side," qualified Emile.

"We're not against your side," clarified Otto.

"But we must seem to be...impartial," explained Mimsy.

Ray grappled with the implications. "So you're not on my
side," he said flatly.

"We did not say that," hastened Emile.

"So, what did you say?" snapped Ray.

"I thought it was clear," said Otto.

"Look," said Ray, with a touch of asperity, "you're either for
me or you're against me."

Mimsy smiled a tolerant, diplomatic smile. "Allow me to agree with you in a slightly different way."

"We're not against you," said Otto.

"But we are not for anyone," said Emile.

"We're for everyone," said Mimsy.

Ray glared at them. "Just give me diplomatic cover. That's all I ask."

The ambassadors traded glances. Then, beaming at Paul, they bowed in formal assent.

"And if that doesn't work," said the Russian Ambassador, Aleksandr Myrmidon, "We are prepared to station missile batteries within the Duchy of Almaviva."

"And give you a bridge loan to cover any expenses you may require," said the Chinese Ambassador, Heidi Ho.

CHAPTER 39

BREAKOUT

Ray and his Almavivans assembled for action. They were about to make the equivalent of Pickett's charge, but this time, they hoped, with better results. For the occasion, Don Raimondo dragged out his ceremonial conquistador armor.

"Oh, no," said Ray. "You're not going to wear that."

"No, I'm not," said Don Raimondo. "You are."

"What!" cried Ray.

"You will, and you must," said Don Raimondo. "You represent the fine old name of Almaviva. I, your ancestor," he said modestly, "not only hijacked the Spanish Treasure Fleet and saved the American Revolution wearing this armor, but remember Gustavo Almaviva, who distinguished himself at the Siege of Toledo in 1090. Or Filiberto Almaviva, who won honors in the Battle of La Rochelle in the Hundred Years' War. Or Rolando Almaviva, who helped Hernan Cortés conquer the Aztec Empire. And Alonso Almaviva, who helped Francisco Pizarro conquer the Incan

Empire. Ray, nine centuries of history look down upon you today. Your ancestors expect you to do your duty."

"I will do my duty," complained Ray, "but do I have to wear that stuff to do it?"

"You do. Do you remember when we met General Washington?" asked Don Raimondo. "I told you that the American revolutionaries needed to recognize our heritage and ronk."

"Not wronk," corrected Ray. "Rank."

"That's what I said," said the First Duke. "The point is that people believe what people see. Our first impression must be inspiring. That is even more important on this day."

"Well, you wear it then," said Ray.

"No, Ray," said Don Raimondo, laying an avuncular hand on Ray's shoulder. "I am the past. You are the future. You are the standard bearer of our family name on this auspicious day."

Don Raimondo had struck a chord, and although it was against his personal wishes, Ray allowed himself to be encased in the ceremonial armor of his noble house. Once suited up, Ray led the Almavivans, under the United Nations flag, toward the Marine checkpoint. There was no more room in the limo, so Ray and the other Almavivans rode alongside it on bicycles.

Back at the White House, McGaffer handed President Haydn a note. The President read it, exuded a bead of sweat, and handed it to General Undershot. "They're breaking out. What are you going to do about it?"

The General's face assumed a hue of outraged purple. "Do about it?" he blustered. "We'll blow the Duchy of Almaviva to cinders; that's what we'll do about it!"

"It may have escaped your notice, General," said McGaffer, "but they're traveling with the Secretary General of the United

Nations."

"There could be a lot of votes in that," volunteered Haydn hopefully. McGaffer and Katrina-Perdue gave him incredulous stares.

"We'll pick 'em off with surgical precision, sir," declared General Undershot, sweeping a chubby hand over the theater of operations map. "Hmm," he added, peering at one sector of the chart.

"What is it?" asked Haydn.

The General stabbed the map with a finger. "That's the Capitol Building, isn't it, sir?"

McGaffer squinted. "Yes."

"Do we spare it?" asked the General.

The President squinted, engaged in an inward struggle. After a long moment of silence, the General repeated: "I said, sir, do we spare it?"

"I'm thinking...," mused the President.

Meanwhile, at the Almavivan checkpoint, the Marine Lieutenant observed Ray, Ilsa, Larry, and Don Raimondo leading a committee of Almavivans and the squadron of ambassadors toward the perimeter fence. One of the MPs said, "Sir, isn't that the woman you told us to arrest?"

The Marine Captain nodded. But his attention was riveted on Ray. He had never seen a combatant so equipped in all his training at Quantico. Ray was sheathed in squeaking conquistador armor and was riding a bicycle. He and the delegation of Ray's neighbors, also on bicycles, flanked the United Nations limo with its twin blue flags. The formation moved slowly forward to challenge the Marine cordon. A Marine Guard asked: "Are we going to shoot them, sir?"

"I don't know," answered the Lieutenant. He pressed his radio button and called, "Checkpoint Charlie to Eagle One."

Back at 1600 Pennsylvania Avenue, a Marine Guard stepped into the Oval Office. "Sir," he said, offering General Undershot the radio.

"Eagle One," replied the Chief of the Joint Chiefs of Staff, pressing the button.

"Sir, they are breaking out," crackled the Lieutenant. "What are our orders?"

"Turn on the TV," barked the General to Daisy.

"Turn on the TV, sir?" asked the Lieutenant, befuddled.

"Not you, Lieutenant!" growled Undershot.

Daisy turned on the TV. Every channel was covering the squad of Almavivans, with Ray leading in conquistador armor, approaching the checkpoint on his bicycle.

"Good God," breathed McGaffer.

"You can't shoot them down," said Daisy, "not on national TV...it would be a PR nightmare."

"PR nightmares are your specialty, aren't they?" said the President acidly.

McGaffer rubbed his chin thoughtfully for a moment. Then he said, "General, let them pass."

"We can't let them pass, sir," rumbled Undershot. "We'll lose face."

"Anyone want to tell me what we *can* do?" exploded the President. There was a moment of embarrassed silence.

"We can put them under arrest," said Undershot.

"Great," scowled McGaffer. "They resist, and the Marines beat up the UN General Secretary, a bunch of ambassadors, and a bunch of unarmed citizens...."

"They're not citizens, sir," said the General. "They're insurrectionists."

"That's not how it will look on TV," said Daisy.

"Let them pass," insisted McGaffer through clenched teeth.

The General stifled indignation, took a deep breath, and pressed the radio button. "Lieutenant: let them pass."

"Yes, sir."

At the checkpoint, the UN limo glided through the perimeter fence. The Marines stood by, boots laced and rifles ready. Ray, in rattling conquistador armor, peddled through on his bicycle. All the Almavivans jumped on their bikes and wobbled forward in his wake. A massive crowd of citizens cheered. "Viva Almaviva!" The Bicycle Armada broke out. The mob showered the Almavivans with confetti and flowers. Carried away, Ray raised a mailed fist, almost losing balance, and shouted, "Cha-a-a-rge!"

The Marine Guard shot a baffled frown at his Lieutenant. "A bicycle charge, sir?" The Lieutenant knit his brows, unable to formulate a comment. Ray and the Almavivan Cavalry pedaled up Pennsylvania Avenue toward the White House.

"Forward, march!" barked the Marine Lieutenant, finally finding his voice. His unit jogged double-time alongside the charge of Almavivan insurrectionists on bicycles. The crowd joined in, trotting along and flinging flower petals in the air. The bird's eye view, captured spectacularly on TV by Monica Bingley in her news copter, brought the President no joy at all.

CHAPTER 40

DAY OF INFAMY

The media had already staked out Lafayette Park, across from the White House, as the logical place for the big news conference with Ray. Ray and his bicycle armada shuddered to a shaky halt below the bronze statue of the Marquis de Lafayette. Don Raimondo gazed up at the statue of his cousin. "Looks nothing like him," he remarked. Then the journalists mobbed Ray. Ilsa intercepted.

"Ladies and gentlemen!" she shouted. "Please!"

The battle ebbed and flowed between Ilsa and the reporters until she got them somewhat in order, and Ray took a stand on the base of Lafayette's statue. Ilsa shouted an introduction. "His Grace...the Duke of Almaviva!"

The crowd went wild with applause. "The American Duke! The American Duke! The American Duke," they chanted. "USA! USA! USA!"

Taking a few folded sheets from her purse, Ilsa handed Ray a typed speech. "Here, Ray," she said. "I thought you might read this."

Ray glanced at the speech. A smile broke across his face. His eyes twinkled as he said: "Ilsa, you're something else."

Ilsa squeezed his hand. "Go get 'em."

Ray drew himself up in grand rhetorical style, and, taking off his morion helmet and holding it under his arm, he glanced at Ilsa's notes and declaimed: "Yesterday, a date which will live in infamy, the Duchy of Almaviva was suddenly and deliberately attacked by armed forces of the Empire of the United States."

Inside the White House, President Haydn and his staff were watching on TV. "Good Lord," gasped McGaffer. "He's using...."

"Almaviva was at peace with that nation," declaimed Ray over the TV. "The facts of yesterday speak for themselves."

"It's...it's FDR's Pearl Harbor speech!" groaned the President.

Outside, in Lafayette Square, Ray continued. "As Commander-in-Chief of the Duchy of Almaviva, I have directed that all measures be taken for our defense. Since this unprovoked and dastardly attack, a state of war has existed between the Duchy and the United States. With confidence in our armed forces...." He gestured to his neighbors, who swelled with pride. "With the unbounded determination of our people..."

The mob shouted: "Almaviva!"

"We will gain the inevitable triumph, so help us God!"

The crowd, including the media, went berserk. They cheered Ray to the echo.

Inside the Oval Office, President Beau Haydn snapped off the TV. Turning to the White House Chief of Staff, he snarled: "Get him in here!"

CHAPTER 41

EN GARDE!

The bevy of ambassadors and Almavivan neighbors expressed their best wishes but stayed behind at Lafayette Square. Ray entered the White House in clanking armor with Ilsa, Larry, and Don Raimondo. As they walked toward the Oval Office, Ilsa stopped cold in front of one of the historic paintings. It was John Trumbull's portrait of Don Raimondo, painted in 1776. She pointed it out to Don Raimondo and Ray. The painting was unfinished, but the family resemblance was striking. "It looks nothing like me," commented Don Raimondo.

As they passed through the metal detector stationed outside the Oval Office, Ray's armor set it off.

"You'll have to remove the armor, sir," said the Marine Guard.

"I will do no such thing," said Ray. "It is my national dress."

"It's all right," McGaffer assured the Marine Guard. "We've cleared it with the Secret Service."

The metal detector bleated as Ray passed through. Don Raimondo paused to inspect the machine, curious as ever at the newfangled inventions of the twenty-first century.

"Come on," urged Ray, annoyed. Inside the Oval Office, the President sat at the Resolute desk. Chief of Staff McGaffer, Press Secretary Katrina-Purdue, Speaker of the House Fanny Villosi, House Minority Leader Kenny McMurphy, Majority Leader of the Senate Jack Boomer, Minority Leader of the Senate Fitch McCormack, Chief Justice of the Supreme Court John Windsock, Secretary of State Wilson Cleaver, Chief of the Joint Chiefs of Staff General Undershot, Don Ricardo, and Luisa Cabana all stood on one side of the room awaiting the Almavivan usurpers. Ray, Ilsa, Larry, and Don Raimondo entered. The team of officials goggled at Ray's conquistador armor. The President cracked his knuckles and assumed an air of campaign-trail affability. "Ray!"

"Beau!" replied Ray.

The President froze. The officials sharply drew breath. McGaffer frigidly intervened.

"Kindly address the President as 'Mr. President.'"

"I think we've been through that," said Ray. "If I do that, then the President must call me 'Your Grace.'"

"Whose Grace?" asked the President.

"His Grace," said Daisy.

"My Grace," said Ray.

McGaffer gritted his teeth.

"Beau will do," said the President.

"This has gone far enough!" hissed Luisa Cabana. "You imposter," she shrilled at Ray. "He is His Grace," she said, pointing a painted nail at Don Ricardo.

"Yes," said Don Ricardo with hidalgo pride, "I am My Grace."

McGaffer appealed to Cleaver. "Who really is His Grace?"

Cleaver said, pointing to Don Ricardo, "Well, the CIA thinks he is His Grace."

Ilsa jumped in, pointing to Ray, "But my research says he is His Grace."

Don Ricardo approached Ray menacingly, nose to nose. Everyone in the room gasped. They were astonishingly identical. They could have been twins. The two men circled each other, inspecting their mirror images critically. Finally, Don Ricardo turned to the others and sneered, "He looks nothing like me."

Then, turning back to Ray, he declared, "There is only one way to settle this honorably." Don Ricardo slipped an Italian leather glove from his belt and arrogantly slapped Ray on the cheek. "Sir," he announced, "I demand satisfaction."

Ray gazed at him in disbelief. Turning to Ilsa, he asked, "Why... did he do that?"

"It is the *Code Duello*," she replied.

"What?"

Don Raimondo came to Ray's aid. "The code of the duel," he explained, "covering the practice of dueling on points of honor. For example, A tells B he is impertinent. B retorts that A lies. A must make the first apology because he gave the first offense; if not, after two shots by both parties, B may explain away the retort by a subsequent apology to A."

"What?" said Ray, fogged.

"I said, A tells B he is impertinent...."

"Hold it!" interrupted Ray. "Am I A or B?"

"B," said Ilsa.

"So what do I do now?"

"You respond to his challenge. Hit him back with a glove."

"I don't have a glove. May I borrow your glove?" he politely asked Don Ricardo.

"No," said Don Ricardo churlishly.

"Now what?" asked Ray.

Ilsa shrugged. "Improvise."

Ray took the metal gauntlet from his arm and slapped Don Ricardo with it, producing a tremendous clang! Don Ricardo tumbled backward over the presidential sofa, with the gaggle of officials gaping in dismay. Don Ricardo struggled to his feet, massaging his bruised jaw. *"O Dios mio!"*

"You barbarian!" shrieked Luisa.

"You have the choice of weapons," Ilsa informed Ray.

"What?" asked Ray.

"You know," said Don Raimondo. "Pistols. Swords. Maces."

"Maces?" inquired Ray.

Ilsa cast an inquiring glance at General Undershot, "I don't suppose we could dig up any maces...?"

General Undershot frowned and shook his head. So, Ray, spying a crossed pair of ceremonial swords on the wall of the Oval Office, drew one and tossed it, pommel first, to Don Ricardo, who instinctively caught it. It was very heavy and plunged Don Ricardo to the carpet with a grunt. He struggled woozily back to his feet. The Secret Service agents dashed to grab the weapon, but again McGaffer stopped them. "It's diplomacy," he explained. The Secret Service didn't like it, but they didn't like a lot of things they had to put up on presidential details.

Ray drew the other sword from the wall and faced his challenger. "We shall settle the matter with honor," said he.

Don Ricardo shot an appealing glance at the flabbergasted President. "I...I will not be bullied in this manner..." he protested.

"En garde!" cried Ray, lunging. The point of his sword pricked

Don Ricardo's chest.

"Ai-yi-yi!" squealed Don Ricardo. He dropped his sword and ran.

"Come back, *mi amor,*" shouted Luisa, bolting after him. The door to the Oval Office slammed shut behind them. Ray plunged his sword into one of the presidential sofas with a satisfying swish.

"To think," said Don Raimondo indignantly, "that such a worm would pretend to bear the proud name of Almaviva."

"You know, I rather like the old feudal ways," Ray said. "Now, Beau," he said, turning to the President.

"Huh?" said Haydn, stunned.

Ray put his arm around the Leader of the Free World. "Call me Ray," he said affably.

McGaffer ripped Ray's arm off the presidential shoulder and glowered at him. "What is it you really want?" he asked.

Ray shot a cue to Larry. Larry handed Ray his petition. Ray snapped it open across the President's desk, and it tumbled out to a gratifyingly dramatic length—about three feet. Ray waved his arms over it, like a wizard conjuring a spell, and grinned at the President with pride. "*Voilà!*"

Chief Justice Windsock picked up the document and began reading. His face went pallid. "This is ridiculous!" he cried.

"As ridiculous as throwing a man in prison unconstitutionally?" asked Larry.

"As ridiculous as building the whole Federal City over a plot of land that was rightfully granted to a hero of the Revolution by legal deed?" asked Ilsa.

"As ridiculous as trying to win the Revolutionary War without gunpowder and bullets? A war that could never have been won without my gold?" said Don Raimondo.

"Uh, our *family's* gold," said Ray, covering for the First Duke.

The Congressional leaders moved in to peruse Ray's list of demands. "Impossible!" cried Speaker Villosi.

"Preposterous!" cried Senator Boomer.

"Absurd!" cried Senator McCormack.

"Interesting," murmured Congressman McMurphy.

"Come," said Ray, "let us reason together. I have a hard cash offer from the Chinese government for the Duchy of Almaviva for one hundred billion dollars. If I sell, every Federal building will be turned into a dim sum palace. If I don't sell, every Federal building and every Federal employee might be allowed to stay."

"Might?" gasped Speaker Villosi.

"On what conditions?" asked Secretary Cleaver.

"Wait, I'm not done. In addition to owning all the land on which Washington, D.C. is squatting, I am owed payment for arrears in hard currency or rent. Accounting for inflation—that would come to much *more* than one hundred billion dollars."

"Would you blackmail your own country?" demanded General Undershot.

"I would treat my country," said Ray suavely, "with the same justice and compassion with which it has treated me. But I am still not done."

"Oh," groaned the President, sinking into his chair.

"You seem to forget that I have been granting citizenship to many Americans."

"How many?" asked Speaker Villosi.

"Fill her in, Larry," said Ray.

Larry cleared his throat, opened his smartphone, and read, "As of last count, 81,282,916. Curiously enough, Mr. President, that is the exact number of votes you supposedly received in the last presidential election. Since those taxpayers are no longer subject to Federal income tax, that subtracts 51.6% of revenue from the Federal government, or about 6.45 trillion dollars."

Senator Boomer turned savagely to Secretary of State Cleaver. "You didn't track all these renounced citizenships?" he hissed.

"We were busy tracking down Don Ricardo," said the Secretary, apologetically.

"And you can't walk and chew gum at the same time?" asked Speaker Villosi.

"They can chew, then take a step, then chew, then take a step, and so on," goaded Congressman McMurphy. "That's about all."

"Tell them the rest," said Ilsa.

Larry continued. "That doesn't take into account all the corporations who have transferred their official residence to the Duchy. To date, eighteen million have done so, which would subtract another 3.6% from the Federal revenue per year. Without considering the fact that passport and business residency applications are still pouring in, you, Mr. President, you, Madam Speaker, you, Mr. Minority Leader, you Mr. Senate Leader, you, Mr. Minority Senate Leader, and you, Chief Justice, are broke."

A grisly silence settled down on the room. Finally, the President summed it up: "Broke."

"Broke," echoed Don Raimondo smugly.

"Now," said Ray, "I have the power to make a deal, and I will make a deal if you will. It will take several acts of Congress and presidential signatures, but you can see all my demands in that document."

"Abolish the IRS?" gulped McGaffer.

"And income tax. And corporate tax," said Ray. "You will just have to fund the government on import duties."

"As we did in my day," said Don Raimondo.

"Your day?" said Speaker Villosi.

"In the past," said Ilsa, covering for Don Raimondo again.

"But what good is making a deal with you to return the national tax base to the Federal government if you are going to abolish Federal taxes?" cried McGaffer.

"What good is not making a deal with me and having me evict the whole District of Columbia as I did the Supreme Court?" asked Ray.

"It wouldn't be good," said Chief Justice Windsock, still licking his wounds.

"Abolish the FBI?" gasped Speaker Villosi, scanning Ray's demands.

"I don't like them," said Ray. "And we don't need a praetorian guard for imperial Washington. I also don't like the CIA, the NSA, and pretty much all the alphabet agencies. If I am going to cede the country back its capital and not sell it to Beijing, you have to shutter them all. You will notice that I also require the closure of all Cabinet departments except Defense, State, and the Treasury."

General Undershot and Secretary Cleaver mopped their brows in relief.

"You would close the Department of Health and Human Services?" wheezed Senator Boomer.

"If you want less of something," said Ray, "you create a Cabinet Department for it. If you want less justice, you have a Department of Justice. If you want less Transportation, you create a department for that. If you want less Commerce, Education, Agriculture, Energy, Housing, and so on, you create departments for those things. Either they all go away, or everyone in Georgetown will have to learn Mandarin."

"You are destroying your country!" shouted Senator Boomer.

"No," thundered Don Raimondo. "He is restoring it. I know. I was there."

Everyone stared at him. Ray slapped his brazen ancestor on the back.

The President sidled up to Ray and slid a campaign-friendly arm around Ray's shoulders. "Why fight us?" he said. "Why not join us? Don't you see? You'd be set for life—fame, money, honor."

"What about principles?" asked Ray.

"Principles," said the President, "aren't what make things work. What works is what makes principles. Don't you see, Ray? People aren't ready to govern themselves. They can't handle freedom. Give the people enough freedom, and they'll always enslave themselves with it. Every time. No, what the people need is leaders like us, visionaries, who know what's good for them."

Ray disentangled himself from Haydn's arm. "Beau," he said coldly, "I am going to make you eat those words. But take your time. Crow is not fast food."

"Your Grace," said McGaffer bitterly, "Machiavelli could have taken your correspondence course."

CHAPTER 42

WINDS OF CHANGE

A few days later, outside the Almavivan checkpoint, the Army Corps of Engineers were vigorously at work, tearing down the barbed wire. A hardhat ambled up to the border and planted a new street sign that read: DUCHY OF ALMAVIVA: FIFTY-FIRST STATE OF THE UNITED STATES OF AMERICA. The hardhat stood back for a moment to admire the sign.

In the White House Rose Garden, President Haydn sat at a desk, signing the last of a tremendous batch of new Congressional Acts. He was flanked by the usual dignitaries. Ray, Ilsa, Larry, and Don Raimondo were at his side. All the Federal officials in the group wore funereal expressions. Turning to the teleprompter, President Haydn oozed: "This is truly a historic moment: The era of Big Government is over...."

Speaker Villosi moaned.

Haydn continued. "The sanctity of the Federal City, Washington, D.C., is forever preserved..."

There was a smattering of feeble applause. The President squinted at the teleprompter and read, "The Duchy of Almaviva is enshrined as the fifty-first state, landlord of the District of Columbia, with the right to send two senators and one representative to Congress...and to be governed by its hereditary Duke, His Grace, Raymond de Borbón y Cortés Almaviva." Senator Boomer sobbed.

"Our long, national nightmare is over," said the President. "I call these Acts that I am signing into law my New, New Deal!" Looking around at the gathering, he beamed expectantly. Crickets. Then Daisy Katrina-Purdue started clapping, and some of the other lackeys of ex-permanent Washington bleakly followed suit. The President flashed a campaign smile for the media and signed the last Act. He gave the historic pen to Ray, who took it with dignified pleasure.

"Hurrah!" the people shouted spontaneously. "The American Duke! The American Duke! Viva Almaviva! USA! USA!" Hats flew in the air. It was not what the President was hoping to hear.

A few days later, outside the FBI Headquarters, a squad of moving men were carrying off a stone sign that read: J EDGAR HOOVER FBI BUILDING. Another squad of moving men brought on another stone sign that read: PALACE OF THE DUCHY OF ALMAVIVA.

Agent Schweppes, angry as a wet cat, tottered down the steps of the ex-FBI building carrying boxes of his personal effects. A disconsolate legion of agents and officials flooded out of the building alongside him. Ray, Don Raimondo, Ilsa, and Larry stood by, watching with a smirk.

"Good day," said Ray to Agent Schweppes, bowing with exaggerated, eighteenth-century courtesy. Schweppes sneered and strode pridefully away, but pride, as they so say, goeth before ... and, in a trice, the erstwhile Special Agent in Charge tripped and sprawled down the steps, his papers and favorite photos flying into the air and scuttling down the sidewalk. Ilsa and Ray laughed. They walked up to the front door of the building, which Ray held courteously open for Ilsa. She smiled, raised an observant eyebrow at his newfound chivalry, and went inside. The foyer was filled with busy workers changing the décor.

"You did it," grinned Ray.

"I did it?" said Ilsa.

"You did, really," said Ray. "You're the one who caused all this trouble."

"You never should have asked me for a date," she smiled.

"Well, aren't you glad I did?" he asked.

"What do you think?" she said, sliding her arm into his.

Ray pulled her near to his side. "It just goes to show you," he said.

"Show me what?" asked Ilsa, flirting.

"How far a little hope can go," said Ray. "Say," he asked, his face drawing near to hers, "are your eyes hurting you?"

"No," replied Ilsa. "Why?"

"Because they're killing me," grinned Ray. And he began a serenade.

SONG: *LET'S LEAD A LIFE TO REMEMBER*

Ray: Some people save for tomorrow.
Others waste away in despair.
Some live in self-imposed sorrow,
With no one to love or to care.

But I want to be your Galahad,
And I want to take you away,
And show you the best times you've ever had,
From now till our last, lovely day.

Ray: Let's lead a life to remember.
Let's give our future a past,
So when we look back in December,
The moonlight of June seems to last.
Let's lead a life so romantic,
That when we are frail and gray,
We'll look back and ponder,
And our grandkids will wonder,
What makes us smile that way.

Ilsa: I won't wait for tomorrow
To live like a millionaire.
There isn't a moment to borrow.
Time isn't lenient or fair.
So I want you to be my Galahad.
And I want to be your bride—
Two sweethearts through times both good and bad,
As into our sunset we ride.

Together: Let's lead a life to remember.
Let's give our future a past,
So when we look back in December,
The moonlight of June seems to last.
Let's lead a life so romantic,
That when we are frail and gray,
We'll look back and ponder,

And our grandkids will wonder:
What makes us smile that way!
We'll make 'em wonder
What makes us smile that way!

Ilsa and Ray laughed. They kissed at last.

CHAPTER 43

BACK TO THE PAST

Back at the apartment, Ray was packing. He was a lot richer now, and he had an actual palace. The former FBI building was horribly ugly and would need a lot of renovation. Still, Emile Débris, the French Ambassador, had promised to bring in architects from Paris who could convert it to something along the lines of Versailles.

"Do you think that will be a bit over the top?" he asked Don Raimondo, who was tinkering with his microwave, turning it on and off.

"What?" asked the First Duke.

"Making the palace like Versailles."

"Of course not," said Don Raimondo with indignation. "You are a duke! Your status demands it. Do you think I risked life and limb and honor for my descendants to live like peasants?"

"You're right, as usual," said Ray.

Don Raimondo put an egg inside the microwave and pushed

the button. It hummed for a few seconds and then gave off a blast like a gunshot. The egg exploded all over the inside of the oven.

"Would you stop that?" said Ray, exasperated.

"I can't help being fascinated by all these machines you have," said Don Raimondo, not in the least repentant. "How does this thing work?"

"I don't know," said Ray. "You push the button, and it works."

"You have too little scientific curiosity," reprimanded Don Raimondo, as he continued to tinker with the device. He put a metal dish inside the microwave and turned it on. Ignoring him, Ray returned to packing, filling up box after box with his vast collection of books. The doorbell rang. He opened the door, and Ilsa swept in, embracing and kissing him. He laughed and kissed her back. Then suddenly, there was a blinding flash from the metal in the microwave. Like lightning, it was followed by a thunderous boom that brought down plaster from the ceiling.

"Was it good for you, too?" asked Ray. But Ilsa was looking over his shoulder in astonishment. Where, a moment ago, Don Raimondo had been standing, there was nothing but scorched tiles and plumes of smoke.

Don Raimondo awoke in a daze. His eyes fluttered uncontrollably. There was a shrill ringing in his ears. But gradually, he recovered his senses and realized that he was sitting in the middle of a road. It was Chestnut Street, right in front of the State House in Old Philadelphia. Horses pulling carriages were stumbling around him. He wobbled to his feet and heard a friendly voice.

"Your Grace!" It was Feliz, his loyal servant.

"Cousin!" It was Lafayette. "Where have you been? And where are our other cousins?"

Don Raimondo blinked at the eighteenth-century buildings of the old capital. Then he laughed and embraced the Marquis and his servant.

"Where did you disappear to?" said Lafayette. "We thought you were dead. I do wish you could have been with us at Yorktown."

"Yorktown?" asked Don Raimondo.

"Yes, Your Grace," said Feliz. "The surrender of the British."

"The British surrendered?" gasped Don Raimondo. "To General Washington?"

"And to the French," said Lafayette with a touch of asperity.

"When?" asked Don Raimondo.

"In October of this year."

"What year?"

"Why, 1781, of course."

"You mean," said Don Raimondo, "the American Revolt, it, it...."

"We won," said Feliz simply.

"And the *victoire*, my dear cousin, was in very large part yours," said Lafayette.

Don Raimondo let out an ecstatic guffaw. "Then it was all worth it!"

"Oh, yes," said Lafayette.

"More than you know," said Don Raimondo, gripping Lafayette by his shoulders, "more than you know, *mon cher cousin!*"

"Well," said the Marquis, "now the winds of change are blowing in France; I am going home. Come with me, *cousin*. Let us bring the banner of liberty, equality, and brotherhood to Europe." Lafayette burst into song.

SONG: *THE RIGHTS OF MAN*

Lafayette: Hurrah for the Rights of Man!

Don Raimondo and Feliz joined him.

All: Equality is nature's plan!
We're created to be free,
And we'll never bend a knee,
But fight for that great birthright,
Our noble, global birthright,
Our birthright since the world began!

CHAPTER 44

TO THE DUKE!

At a gala reception in the Palace of Almaviva, Ray, the Duke, and Ilsa, his consort and future Duchess, received a host of celebrities. Although not finished, the palace was already showing signs of noble grace, and as the guests entered the grand double doors into the marble foyer facing a sweeping staircase, Larry, acting as majordomo, took the cards of the guests and announced them.

"His Excellency, President Beau Haydn, and First Lady Jane Haydn."

The President, flanked by his Secret Service detail, staggered into the room and veered off in the wrong direction. The First Lady took him by the shoulders and steered him back toward Ray, who, dressed in a tuxedo with a ducal sash, received the Leader of the Free World.

"Mr. President," said the Duke.

"Your..."

"Grace," said the First Lady.

"Your Grace," repeated the President.

"The Honorable Speaker of the House of Representatives, Fanny Villosi," boomed Larry. "The Honorable Majority leader of the Senate, Jack Boomer. The Honorable Minority Leader of the House of Representatives, Kenny McMurphy. The Honorable Minority Leader of the Senate, Fitch McCormack. The Honorable Chief Justice of the Supreme Court, John Windsock. Her Excellency, the Secretary General of the United Nations, Dr. Mimsy Borogrove. His Excellency, the French ambassador, Monsieur Emile Débris. Her Excellency, the ambassador from the United Kingdom, Heather McFly. His Excellency, the German ambassador, Otto Zeufer. Her Excellency, the Chinese ambassador, Heidi Ho. His Excellency, the Russian ambassador, Aleksandr, Myrmidon. And Dean of the History Department at our esteemed university, Dr. Bradford M. Bradford."

"That's *Dr. Dr.* Bradford M. Bradford," corrected Bradford. "I'm a double Ph.D."

As each dignitary entered, Ray graciously received them, condescending, despite his noble title, to shake hands. Ilsa stood proudly at his side. She fancied she was as pretty now, in her diamond tiara, in an aristocratic sort of way.

Monica Bingley and her cameraman, along with a gaggle of journalists, also flooded in. Once the guests had assembled, the palace wine butler gave a signal, and twenty footmen circulated, offering crystal chalices of chilled champagne to everyone. On their silver trays, they displayed the bottle with the proud label, *"Chateau Almaviva, Méthode Champenoise."*

When everyone had taken a chalice, the Duke solemnly raised his glass. "To the American Dream!"

"The American Dream," said all in chorus.

There was a historic slurp, as the whole assembly sipped as if with a single pair of lips.

Then the President proposed a toast. Lifting his glass, he said, "We hold these truths to be self-evident: all men and women are created by—you know, you know, the thing. America is a nation that can be defined in a single word: Asufutimaehaehfutbw."

Everyone in the room stared at everyone else in bewilderment. The President, however, took a sip of his champagne as if he had delivered a remark that would live forever in Bartlett's *Familiar Quotations*, which probably, in fact, it would. Shrugging, everyone took another sip as well.

"You know, Ray," confided Beau Haydn genially, sidling up to the Duke, "you almost tore apart the greatest country in the world."

The murmur of the crowd ceased at this breach of etiquette. There was pin-drop silence. Ray set down his champagne.

"With all due respect, Mr. President," he retorted icily, "I think maybe we are finally putting it back together."

Haydn affably patted Ray's back. "Well, we were always on the same side, really, Ray. The people's side." With a sweep of his hand, he wrote imaginary headlines in the sky. "You know, my New, New Deal."

"You know," Ray bristled, "I never liked that, Beau. I mean, who are you to give the American people deals?"

"I beg your pardon," said the President.

"Ilsa," said Ray, turning to her, "what would the Founding Fathers think if they knew that in America today, you need a license to drive, a license to fish, a license to sell beer, a license to practice law, or a license to run a business? What would they think?"

"I don't think they would have paid for licenses to do any of those things," said Ilsa.

"No!" said Ray. "They'd have fought it with gunpowder and blood! And what do the people get out of all these licenses of yours?" he asked Haydn. "Nothing. The fees just fund more agencies to issue more licenses to collect more fees. The only way you know how to cut red tape is lengthwise."

"That's hardly fair," protested Speaker Villosi.

"If you were a fish," asked Ray, "would you feel better about being gaffed if you knew the fisherman had a license? You know," he added, "we Americans were trading our God-given rights for a mess of food stamps. Mr. President," he said, turning to Haydn, "I know what George Washington would have done with half the bureaucrats in this town. He'd have given them a blindfold and a cigarette made with tobacco from his own farm!"

The First Lady, Jane Haydn, was aghast. She set her champagne flute down with a trembling hand. "That sounds," she said darkly, "like the campaign speech of someone planning to run for...high office...."

"Not a bad idea!" exclaimed Ilsa, slipping her arm inside Ray's.

Haydn began to unravel. "Is that your game, Ray?" he gargled. "You wouldn't dare! You know I'm running for a second term, and we have a treaty!"

Ray smiled. "There's nothing in the treaty about that."

"But...but..." spluttered the President.

"Don't worry, Mr. President," smiled Ilsa. "What is on our horizon right now is a honeymoon...."

She kissed Ray. The press cameras flashed.

Mopping his brow in relief, the President panted, "Congratulations."

"Thank you," smiled Ray, holding Ilsa close.

"And," said the Leader of the Free World, "take as long a

honeymoon as you possibly can...!"

"Yes, Mr. President!" laughed Ilsa. "Because life, I've learned, isn't just about planning for the future. It's also about using the present to create a beautiful past." Turning to Ray, she took his hands, gazed into his eyes, and sang. As she did so, the ducal orchestra struck up the band.

SONG: *LET'S LEAD A LIFE TO REMEMBER*

Ilsa: Let's lead a life to remember.
Let's give our future a past...

Ray: So when we look back in December,
The moonlight of June seems to last.

Beau Haydn, his mood easily altered, swayed to the music. Soon, so did everyone else in the room.

Together: Let's lead a life so romantic,
That when we are frail and gray,
We'll look back and ponder,
And our grandkids will wonder,
What makes us smile that way.

Now everyone in the room sang in chorus.

Let's lead a life to remember.
Let's give our future a past,
So when we look back in December,
The moonlight of June seems to last.
Let's lead a life so romantic,
That when we are frail and gray,
We'll look back and ponder,
And our grandkids will wonder:

What makes us smile that way!
We'll make 'em wonder
What makes us smile that way!

And then Ray sang another song, one of long ago. The orchestra changed key and played along.

SONG: *THE RIGHTS OF MAN, FINALE*

Ray: Oh, there's a whiff of something different in the air.

Ilsa: You can't see it, you can't touch it, but it's there.

Ray: For the globalist elite
Are going down to a defeat,

Larry: And freedom is reviving everywhere!

Overcome with exuberance, Monica Bingley chimed in.

Monica: Oh, we are bringing back the freedom of the press!

Larry: And shutting down the FBI and IRS!

Ray: For today the people's creed
Is that the only thing we need
To bring about our nation's happiness–

[Spoken] Is–

Ray, Ilsa, Larry, and Monica sang in four-part harmony.

All Four: Respect for the Common Man!
For liberty is nature's plan!
And it's time to take a romp
Through this bureaucratic swamp

And flush out every creature that we can!

The tune was so patriotic and catchy, the whole assembly joined in.

> All: Hurrah for the Rights of Man!
> Equality is nature's plan!
> We're created to be free,
> And we'll never bend a knee,
> But fight for that great birthright,
> Our noble, global birthright,
> Our birthright since the world began!

They all take a deep breath for the grand finale in a slower, grander tempo.

> All: We will never, never rest
> Until everyone is blessed
> With that noble birthright,
> Our noble, global birthright,
> Our birthright since the world began!

The End

Epilogue

"History does not repeat itself,
but it often echoes."

—Mark Twain